Whisper Island

BY

PAMELA MOULTON

Whisper Island

Writing as Pamela Moulton

For permission requests, contact Pamela Willmoth at pam.willmoth@ gmail.com.

ISBN: 978-1-7378556-8-2 (Paperback)
ISBN: 978-1-7378556-9-9 (eBook)

Incubation Press

First Edition 2026

For Jen –

Most of us have, at one time or another, come to realize that life is full of unexpected twists. I was lucky enough to meet you when we were both working on our second acts. The memories of our collective wins and losses, and especially the laughter, will stay with me forever. Cheers, my friend; here's to a life fully lived! And a shoutout to Philadelphia, the amazing city that continues to host our friendship.

Prologue

The wind was really blowing. Mike leaned forward on his bike, trying to create as little resistance as possible while he caught his breath. He'd pushed himself up the steep incline of Eagle Nest. Now he could cruise for a short distance before enjoying the sensation of free-fall while riding down that same steep slope. He brushed the dark hair out of his eyes and noticed his breath flowing in and out and slowing down now that he was on the level ground of the summit.

He felt at peace today. Pushing himself physically always brought him at least some degree of calm, but today it was more than that. The peace came from knowing that he had made up his mind. He'd spent many months agonizing over how his decision would affect the two most important people in his life—Rheagan and Greg. He knew they loved him and were in his corner unconditionally; he just wished things were different. *I wish I could be different.* He had wavered on this decision more times than he could stand, but now he was certain that he'd made the right choice for his future. He nosed his bike to the edge of the summit, just past the stop sign. With one quick shove, he embraced the rush of the wind as gravity propelled him down the hill.

Chapter One

Rheagan opened the coat closet, reaching for her usual yellow rain jacket, and then stopped and selected the navy blue one instead. *Yellow feels too bright for today.* With a sigh, she zipped the darker jacket over her gray sweater. Grabbing her purse, she opened her front door. She rattled the doorknob to ensure the apartment door was ready to lock behind her before turning down the long corridor that led to the exit of her building. She passed her business office, and through the window in the door, she saw papers neatly stacked on the desk awaiting her attention. Mike's office was next, but she averted her eyes from the closed door, keeping her gaze fixed on the stairs and the outside door at the bottom of them. She paused only long enough to pull up her jacket's hood to cover her hair from the Northwest drizzle before opening the door and breathing in the cool, damp air. The smell was a familiar mix of seaweed and marine life. She closed her eyes, filled her lungs, and exhaled deeply to calm her nerves.

Even though it was not yet 9:00 a.m., Main Street was relatively busy. She stood for a moment, absorbing the familiarity and welcoming comfort of Belle Harbor, the area where she lived and worked. The mom-and-pop storefronts were dressed in colorful striped awnings and window boxes of spring flowers. The anemones, also called windflowers, were her personal favorites. She watched the colorful blossoms in reds, yellows, pinks, and whites bend and lean in the drizzle and chilly morning air. Somehow, the delicate flowers always managed to regain their upright posture. *Maybe I can borrow some strength from them …*

Rheagan shook her head, clearing her thoughts. *I need to get going.* She considered stopping at The Coffee Bean for a soy latte, but wasn't sure she had time to stand in a long line of morning customers. She also wasn't sure she was up for facing her friend Kate's sympathetic gaze. Kate knew she was signing the papers today. Instead, Rheagan decided to walk directly to Greg's law office. She could already see the newly renovated building that had preserved the clapboard wood look of the waterfront district. After she climbed the stairs to his spacious office, his assistant Nan would offer her a cup of coffee.

It was there, a coffee cup clutched in her hand, that Greg saw her. She was sitting in the tobacco-colored leather chair across from his desk, her body turned toward the window, her eyes fixed on the choppy gray waters of Puget Sound. She must have heard him in the doorway because she turned and stood, facing him with a wobbly smile. He walked directly to her and put his arms around her, hugging her tightly. He smelled her subtle floral scent and felt the silkiness of her long auburn hair brush against his fingers. He sensed her shoulders shaking and knew that she had begun to cry. He pulled her slender body in for one more hug, then stepped back and reached for the box of tissues Nan always kept on his desk. Rheagan accepted one gratefully and sank back into her chair, dabbing at her eyes and nose.

"I know neither of us wants to be doing this today. Do you need some time?" Greg seated himself in the chair beside her rather than the one behind his desk. He focused his attention on her watery, caramel-colored eyes as if they might provide a better assessment than any words she might say.

He saw that she took a deep breath, but she met his gaze directly, and her voice was soft but determined. "I'm ready."

Greg nodded, "Okay, as you know, our attorney Bill will conduct the meeting via Zoom. I have the original documents here, including the life insurance policy. Mike put a lot of effort into making sure you wouldn't lose Savor. He knew how much the restaurant means to you." He opened a file and handed her several pages, keeping a few for himself.

Rheagan nodded, accepting the documents without looking at them.

Greg wasn't surprised—she knew what they contained. Mike had been adamant that the three of them have their business interests clearly defined and protected in the event of an "unforeseen occurrence." As an attorney himself, Greg had agreed with Mike's request, and Rheagan hadn't been opposed. *Being prepared and actually dealing with the reality of an "unforeseen occurrence" are two very different things.* He forced his attention away from the woman beside him and back to the present as the Zoom meeting opened and Bill's face appeared on the screen.

Forty-five minutes later, the meeting participants had completed their review of the business interest valuation and the secured financing terms. After agreeing to the funding process, Rheagan and Greg executed the buy/sell documents that had been put in place by the three partners, and Greg set aside the original papers to send to Bill's Seattle law firm.

Bill looked directly into his computer's camera. "Rheagan, I know this is a tough situation, and I'm sorry this process has been so long for you. This case was as straightforward as they come, but the probate courts are currently backlogged, and everything is being delayed. I want to assure you that the steps taken today should provide peace of mind. With your buyout of Mike and Greg's respective interests in your restaurant, Savor, you are now the sole owner. I hear it's now one of the best restaurants on the island." Bill smiled gently. "I wish you all the best," he said with compassion and professionalism. Rheagan nodded, thanking him for his assistance.

Greg reached forward and clicked the button on the screen to end the call before turning back to face Rheagan. "I have an additional document to review with you," he said, focusing again on her eyes to measure her mental state. They still reflected sadness, weariness, and now a degree of wary surprise. He reached for a file on his desk and handed her a document—another life insurance policy.

She scanned it, seeing her name as the beneficiary and the amount of $500,000. Her head snapped up, her eyes meeting Greg's surprised and concerned hazel eyes, and then her slim body sank back into the chair as tears flowed freely down her cheeks.

"Rheagan, what's wrong? Why are you so upset?" Greg had not expected a negative reaction from her, and certainly not of this magnitude. "Mike and I discussed this. We didn't realize the day would come so soon, but he wanted you to have some extra financial room."

"Greg, it's just too much! What we just signed is already overwhelming. The first policy was enough to reimburse you for the money you fronted us for Savor. And now this? It feels wrong to be gaining financially from Mike's death!"

Greg saw what looked like panic in her expressive eyes, and he reached for her hand, holding it tightly. "Rheagan, Mike loved you. He wanted you to have options. He knew that you moved here to Whisper Island for him. He wanted to know that you would have enough financial security to decide your future on your terms."

Rheagan nodded, sniffling and wiping at her eyes with the crumpled tissue, but Greg thought he could still see alarm in her eyes. Then she gathered herself, her lips turning up in a smile that didn't match her sad eyes, "Mike loved you, too. I may have moved to Whisper Island for him, but he wanted to be here with you. He always said your friendship changed his life."

Greg nodded and ran his fingers through his dark blond hair before answering. "I loved him like a brother, and I was thrilled when he decided he liked it here, since I'd always known I would come back for good after college. This island is my home. What about you, Rheagan? Will you stay?"

"I'm still not sure of anything right now," she said quietly.

Chapter Two

Balancing her soy latte and a toasted bagel with cream cheese, Rheagan walked from the city center and sat on her regular bench in the small park along the harbor. The bench faced Sea Lion Perch, an outcropping of large, black, craggy rocks that was a favorite sunning spot for the resident sea lions, seals, and even the occasional otter. Her yellow rain jacket hood was pulled up to protect her from the chilly morning drizzle. Today, the gray water was calm, gently lapping the rocks, and the air carried the scent of rotten eggs, likely from decaying organic matter in the water. Rheagan loved the whole experience.

Whenever time allowed, this was how she started her day. She had given the regular mix of sea lions and seals individual names and tried to identify them on her visits. Today, Brutus, the large, gray-spotted sea lion, was taking up the majority of the space. His usual sea lion cronies, Max and Sporty, crowded together on the same rock to find a spot out of the water. She watched as Rocky the intrepid seal tried to find a perch, and she leaned forward, squinting to see better. *Wait, is that Rocky?* Her secret shame was that she might be misidentifying Rocky; the seals were definitely more challenging to recognize. With a reluctant wave goodbye to her marine mammal friends, she wiped the crumbs from her lap and prepared to return to her office. She had needed this respite, but she couldn't delay any longer.

Has it really been eight months since the accident? It still didn't even feel real that a tourist's car had randomly hit Mike, killing him instantly. *It's all been such a blur, and I can still barely pull myself together.* Seated at her office desk, Rheagan smoothed the papers from the prior day's meeting. She tried to absorb the knowledge that she was now the sole owner of the restaurant she and Mike had built together. Both of them had immediately loved the site, and it was hard to beat the quaint Main Street for both tourist and local traffic, so Rheagan had used an inheritance from her grandmother to purchase the quirky building. She and Mike had modernized the small ground-floor restaurant and created a two-bedroom apartment plus an office for each of them on the top floor. It had been hard work, but also rewarding. Greg's investment had enabled them to complete the renovations and get the restaurant off the ground. *It was my dream come true—I'd always wanted to own a restaurant. But now …* With one finger, she traced the amount of the surprise life insurance policy on the papers in front of her and squeezed her eyes tightly shut. She wasn't ready to think about that right now.

She opened a desk drawer, filed the papers neatly away, and extracted a key. It was time, well past time, but she wasn't strong enough to do it alone. Dropping the key in her pocket, she left her office, heading down the hall to her apartment. *It still feels weird, calling this "my" apartment—it was supposed to be Mike and me here forever.* As she unlocked the door, she heard a soft meow, and Mr. Pickles, her recently adopted orange tabby, came racing down the hallway to greet her. Losing traction on the slippery wood floor, he came to a sudden bump and an undignified tumble over her boot. Rheagan smothered a laugh while bending down to scoop him up. She kissed the top of his head and, holding him tightly, headed back down the hall. Just like he'd made her apartment less lonely, Mr. Pickles was going to help her face Mike's office.

Fitting the key in the door, she pushed it open and stepped inside the cluttered room. The air felt stale, as untouched spaces often do. She'd only been in this room once since the accident to get what she had needed for day-to-day operations. Since then, she'd tried to ignore its existence. *Probably not the best choice. Is it going to be any easier now, or like pulling a scab off a wound?* She slowly put the squirming Mr. Pickles on the floor, walked to Mike's desk, and settled into his chair. Breathing deeply, she forced herself to just *be* in the space. With her eyes closed, she could picture Mike there, pacing back and forth, gesturing with his coffee cup, filled with ideas and that restless energy of his.

Like her own office, Mike's office had a large window, allowing for plenty of daylight. The similarities ended there. While Rheagan's office reflected her organized and perhaps manic neatness, Mike's office was an explosion of colorful chaos. His desktop was randomly layered with culinary magazines and worn cookbooks, and even more books and magazines leaned in crooked stacks on the floor. Large pegboards covered his wall, filled with glossy pictures of food—succulent roasts, elegant pork loins, mouth-watering desserts. Rheagan knew those pictures had likely inspired the dishes that were currently on the Savor menu. Even with all the clutter, there were no personal items on his desk, and when she opened the desk drawers, she found them empty. Mike had used this space as a staging area for his role as head chef, but he had spent most of his time in the kitchen, his happy place.

Rheagan felt tension in her shoulders, realizing that this visit was not going as planned. She had expected reclaiming his office to add another layer of sadness. It would feel like another step toward letting him go from her life. But now, being in Mike's office, she grasped that this space felt far less personal than what she had already endured—sleeping in their shared bed and removing his things from their living space. Instead, reclaiming this space would push her to step up and take the lead to keep the restaurant thriving.

She took several deep breaths, exhaling slowly, willing the panic to subside. She reached for Mr. Pickles and pulled him onto her lap, where he purred quietly as she scratched under his soft, fuzzy chin. She sat there in the silence, wanting to feel even a flicker of reassurance, but none was forthcoming.

She had grown up in her parents' pizza restaurant, and working with food was in her blood. Running a restaurant was as natural as breathing. *So why am I struggling? Running my own successful restaurant is my dream, right?*

As she sank deeper into Mike's old office chair, she realized she'd been in denial and not taking on actual ownership and responsibility for Savor's future. She'd just been going through the motions, performing her usual role as executive chef, handling both business and financial functions and front-of-house operations. All the while, she'd been acting as if Mike were still performing his role as the creative mind behind menus and the hands-on head chef.

She felt a burning shame for her neglect of Savor and how that must be impacting Joe, her sous chef. She knew she had not given him the support he needed as he attempted to fill the void left by Mike. *Joe deserves better, and Savor deserves better. What is wrong with me?*

She sat still, forcing herself to face her failure. *I'm not sure I deserve Savor.*

Chapter Three

As Greg opened the front door to The Coffee Bean, he sniffed appreciatively at the aroma of roasted beans in the cozy cafe. He saw Rheagan sitting at a corner table with a latte in front of her and a black coffee waiting for him. She was dressed casually in jeans and a sweatshirt, her long auburn hair pulled back into a ponytail that highlighted the delicate bone structure of her face. Since the accident, they had made it a monthly habit to grab a coffee. Mike would have wanted him to check in on her, but the truth was, Greg looked forward to spending time with her. Today, he especially wanted to see her because he'd been concerned about her since their recent meeting in his office. He wanted to make sure she was okay. This morning, he knew he'd interrupted her shopping for restaurant provisions, and as he got closer, he saw that she had a cloth bag filled with fresh herbs on the chair beside her.

He reached down to kiss her cheek before taking his seat. "Thank you for the coffee, but it was my turn to treat."

"The next two are definitely on you," she said with a straight face, and they shared a smile.

He reached over, grabbing her hand and squeezing it. "How is your morning going?"

"I'm good, Greg. I mean that. I've done a lot of thinking, especially last night. I had been avoiding Mike's office, but yesterday I spent some time in there, and realized I've been in denial. I guess it's all just another step in the process, but I'm finally ready to step up and do more to keep Savor on track."

Again, he focused on her eyes because he believed the saying that the eyes were the window to the soul. Her eyes were sad, but maybe he saw a sign of acceptance there as well. With the ownership agreement completed, hopefully, she could start moving forward.

"You have a very intense expression," Rheagan said, interrupting his internal rumination.

Greg's laugh lines crinkled at the corners of his eyes as he grinned, but his expression was sheepish. "You caught me—I have a habit of looking at eyes to see if they mirror the sentiments people express verbally."

Rheagan rewarded him with a smile that brought her delicate features to life, revealing the dimples on her cheeks. "And … How did I do?"

"Not fair, the dimples throw me off," Greg responded, laughing. *And that you have the slightest of freckles crossing the bridge of your nose …* Shaking his head, he changed the subject and asked, "So how is the restaurant business going?"

Rheagan paused. "The community has been incredible. They have supported Savor and been so kind . I know I need to do more, and I hope I'm ready—I think I just felt numb for so long …" Her voice trailed off, and she seemed to turn inward.

Greg broke the silence. "Rheagan, go easy on yourself. You're dealing with a lot." He smiled a welcome to someone behind her, and then Kate, the owner of The Coffee Bean, pulled up a chair, her blonde curls pulled back with a yellow headband featuring the cafe's logo.

Kate hugged Rheagan warmly and squeezed Greg's shoulder before taking her seat. "I hope you don't mind if I join you. It's such a nice surprise to see the two of you sitting in for a change instead of taking out. I guess I have the rain to thank for that!" The conversation shifted to local news about the island, and Kate's lively personality and warm nature brought out a few smiles from Rheagan, along with her dimples.

Greg was glad to see Rheagan relaxed and smiling. *Maybe it's just my imagination that she seems stressed about something more than she's admitting. I think I'll suggest that we meet weekly so I can check in on her more often.*

Chapter Four

Rheagan pushed open the back employee entrance to Savor and was barely in the door before Joe was beside her to relieve her of the overflowing bags of fresh produce. He wore his long brown hair pulled back with a band, and a red bandana was tied across his forehead. As usual, his focus was entirely on his craft and the produce she had brought. Glancing over at him, she saw him with new appreciation. He had been the steady and talented partner she had depended on since Mike's death. Together, they began laying out the raw ingredients on the stainless-steel counter.

"The carrots look beautiful today. These will work well if we roast them whole, leaving a little of the top green. The bigger ones we can use for the mirepoix," Joe murmured as he moved to inspect the cremini and baby portobello mushrooms, shallots, and celery. Trey, one of the line cooks, joined them in unpacking more of the produce.

"Lou will be by shortly to deliver the salmon and halibut from his catch. Oh, and before I forget, here is the fresh basil you requested." Rheagan pulled the cloth bag from the chair where she had laid her yellow jacket. "When you get a moment, Joe, will you join me upstairs in my office?"

"Sure, give me five minutes," Joe replied, his attention still focused on inspecting and sorting through the selections on the table.

Upstairs, Rheagan opened Mike's office door and then went back to her own to review some paperwork while she waited. A few minutes later, she heard the security system beep, telling her that the door to the back internal staircase had been opened with Joe's fob. At the sound of his arrival, she stepped out into the hall and, with a determined smile, waved him into Mike's office. "I've decided it's time to use this room again." Rheagan sighed as she sat in one of the two chairs across from the desk and gestured for Joe to take the other.

Joe stood still for a moment, looking around the colorful room. "You know, I keep expecting him to come around a corner." He shook his head, "Man, I miss him—he was an amazing chef. I learned a lot from him."

Rheagan smiled gratefully. "I know … and, Joe, I want to thank you for stepping up to fill Mike's role these last few months. I couldn't have done it without you, and I want to apologize for being selfish in this process. I feel as if I put a lot of pressure on you. While you haven't let me down, I'm not sure it's been fair to you."

Joe shook his head as if to disagree with her, but Rheagan gave him a sad smile and shook her own head. "No, Joe, I need to say this—I am proud of you and the chef you are today. I also want to help you grow and further develop your skills. We used to change the specials routinely, and I know that hasn't happened since Mike's passing. I want to collaborate with you to brainstorm new dishes and refresh existing ones. Are you up for this?"

Joe's immediate smile was contagious, and Rheagan felt her own lips turn up. He stilled and cocked his head to the side.

She had noticed that he always did that when he was deep in thought. "Rheagan, you showed faith in me that I could step up, and I appreciate that more than you know. And you did adjust my comp, which was also appreciated," he said, smiling again. "I would like the opportunity to work with you more closely. I enjoyed the times you gave Mike a break and worked the back of the house. I learned a lot from watching how you improvised during stressful times."

"I'm not sure I know what you mean," Rheagan said.

"Well, in the kitchen, you seem to sense when things are starting to veer off, and you can bring them back under control." He shrugged. "The kitchen staff were always more at ease when you were back with us."

"Hmm, interesting." Rheagan nodded and then laughed softly. "Mike did like to yell."

"Oh yeah," Joe added, smiling broadly.

"Joe, I want you to know that I intend to promote you to head chef once I get my hands fully around the business finances. Mike's life insurance helped me to cover the funding Greg had provided for Savor, but I need to spend some time making sure I have all my bases covered."

Joe's brown eyes brightened, and she saw what looked like a flash of surprise, but when he replied, his tone was respectful and even. "Thank you, Chef. I would love that opportunity when the time is right."

"All right, well, I've taken enough of your time, Joe. I'm going to clean up this space and make it more functional for us. And I'll be reaching out soon to start that brainstorming process on the menu." She stood up from her stool. "Oh, Joe, we should also be thinking about the next sous chef. Do you think it should be Trey or Manny?"

Again, Joe stilled and cocked his head to the side. "My initial thought is Trey. He is perhaps more technical at this point, but let me give it more thought."

He turned as if to head back to the kitchen, but then stopped, his expression looking troubled. "Chef, I don't want to be an ass, but I caught Manny taking some basil home with him. It could have messed up our inventory, so I thought I should say something. Anyway, that's why I asked you to get some more basil this morning. He's a good guy, and maybe it was the first and only time? I'm happy to talk to him, but I wanted to let you know first."

"I've got it, given all the changes we've had, but normally this would fall in your venue," Rheagan said, smiling reassuringly at him. "I grew up in this business, and good employees are hard to find. Manny is a good guy—I agree with you. Let me figure out what the story is. I appreciate the heads up." Joe nodded and headed back to the kitchen. Rheagan took a deep breath. *Handling the basil situation is the easy part.*

Chapter Five

Back in her office, Rheagan hit the *Submit Payment* button on the last invoice and filed her paperwork neatly away. Glancing at her watch, she realized that somehow, she had managed to get ahead of schedule. She could start reorganizing Mike's office.

After her initial visit to the space with Mr. Pickles and her meeting with Joe earlier today, she knew that Mike's office, as it was currently set up, would not work for her. Whether that was because it couldn't actually function for her or that she just needed to make it her *own* space, she wasn't sure, and she didn't want to think too deeply about it.

She pushed the door open with her hip and set the two empty boxes she'd been carrying beside his desk. Her idea was to put all the pictures and books in a box for her and Joe to look through later. She wanted to remove the desk, envisioning in its place a long, rectangular worktable, along with pictures on the wall and plants to bring the room to life. *A space to inspire creativity needs a little design pizazz of its own.*

As she removed the last stack of books from the now-empty floor, she recognized a study manual from the CIA, the culinary school where Mike and she had met. She opened the manual, and the sight of his familiar handwriting in the margins and scrawled notes throughout brought tears to her eyes. She sat down heavily in his chair. *This book is the most personal item I've found among Mike's things.*

Living with Mike, she had never known him to be sentimental, a fact proven true when she'd cleaned out his possessions from their home after his accident. She had found no pictures, cards, silly handwritten notes—not even ones she had sent him. Mike had told her early on that he was an only child and that his mother had been ill much of her life. After she'd died of cancer in his senior year of high school, he just wanted to start his life over. Nostalgia was a complex emotion for him, and he preferred to live in the present, he had explained. *But wasn't I someone to feel nostalgic about?*

Rheagan felt a wave of anxiety wash over her, and she took a deep breath to tamp it down. *I have been surviving his death by only focusing on the day-to-day. Now, I am getting deeper into the business side … Soon, I will have to deal with the personal side on a deeper level, too.* Wiping at a tear, she laid the manual back on the desk, and a small gold key fell from between the pages. *I wonder what this is for?* she thought as she examined it. Noticing the time, she saw that if she wanted to stay on schedule, she needed to shower and dress for her evening role, which included being front of the house, bartender, and so on. She set the gold key beside the manual and left the office.

By 9:45 p.m., the last guests had departed, and Rheagan and the staff were in cleanup and restocking mode. When Rheagan finished balancing her cash register, she stood for a moment appreciating how the darkness outside the windows made the

interior of Savor look intimate and charming. She focused on the freshly mopped wide-plank hardwood floors, their dark stain similarly reflected in the overhead wooden ceiling beams. She appreciated the contrast of the newly laid white tablecloths, fresh candles, and gleaming table settings. *When was the last time I really let myself appreciate Savor?*

She turned out the lights and headed to the kitchen to find Manny. She saw him and Trey working together, wrapping the leftover produce in Saran Wrap, then stacking it on trays for storage in the cooler. "Looking good, guys." Rheagan gestured at the kitchen.

"Chef," Manny said, smiling as she approached.

"Hey, Manny, I could use your help tomorrow for an hour, maybe a little more. First thing in the morning would be best. Can you talk to Joe and make sure he can spare you?"

"Sure thing, Chef. Is there something I can help you handle tonight? I could stay late if needed." He handed the last of the produce to Trey, who headed into the cooler to organize everything.

"Thanks, Manny, but we can't do it tonight. Tomorrow morning, the hardware store is delivering six large planters and some soil. I thought you could go with me to Orcas Farms. I plan to select various herbs and start growing them here at Savor. Joe and I are going to collaborate on revamping some of our existing dishes and developing new ones. Since I don't yet know what direction we may go in, I want different herb choices on hand."

Manny nodded, but his energy seemed to have depleted, and his eye contact slid away from hers. Rheagan heard him sigh, and then he met her eyes again. "Chef, I took some basil home Tuesday night. I shouldn't have done it without asking, and I swear it was the only time."

Before Rheagan could respond, he began speaking again, his tone earnest and his brown eyes pleading for her understanding. "I know I screwed up. I didn't think about the fact that the inventory count would be off the next morning and that we could end up being short for orders because of my actions. I saw that you had to buy more the next day."

Rheagan nodded, holding his gaze. "That's the real issue, Manny. We depend on an accurate inventory when we do our morning shopping. Why did you want the basil?" she asked.

Manny looked miserable, but he still looked her in the eye. "Chef, I wanted to show off to my girl and make basil-arugula pesto over pasta for her, but the grocery store didn't have any basil, not even the bad shit cut up in those little containers. Chef, I have learned to appreciate fresh herbs through my work here. Chef, I'm sorry."

Rheagan fought to keep a straight face. "Thanks for the apology, Manny. Joe saved the day by double-checking in the morning before I went to the farm, so I was able to stop by the greenhouse and get some more. In the future, ask before you take, and keep that inventory count accurate! That said, I feel the same way about fresh herbs, so the pots I ordered are large and there should be room for sharing." She gave his arm a light punch as she turned to go, calling over her shoulder, "Clear it with Joe, and I'll find you in the morning."

"Yes, Chef!" he answered, and she could hear the relief in his voice.

Upstairs in her cozy apartment, she poured herself an oversized glass of pinot noir, wrapped herself in a soft throw on the couch, and acknowledged that the emotional protections she had built to distance herself from both her personal and business lives were indeed beginning to crumble. Tonight, she allowed herself to miss just being with Mike. They would have laughed together about the basil incident, knowing that the actual *borrowing* was immaterial, but it was the ability to turn it into a teachable moment that counted. *Well ... maybe a teachable moment was a little outside of Mike's emotional makeup. Still, the look on Manny's face!* Mr. Pickles startled her by jumping into her lap, and she cuddled his warm, purring body, thankful that she wasn't completely alone. She was still getting used to the stillness of her apartment without Mike's restless presence.

She finished her wine and moved into her bathroom to brush her teeth and wash her face. Her thoughts kept spinning with the events of the last few days—becoming the sole owner of Savor, realizing she'd been stalling, and needing to step up as a leader. *At least I'm trying to meet the challenges, reclaim Mike's office, and engage Joe on the menu.* She acknowledged the onslaught of feelings—sorrow, pride, and, of course, guilt. Still, when she looked at herself in the mirror, she saw her reflection with new clarity and even a measure of optimism.

Chapter Six

Greg watched the Seattle city skyline out the window as the waters of Lake Washington drew closer and closer, and the seaplane prepared to land. *This is one of those things that never gets old,* he thought as he caught a glimpse of a cormorant diving into the water for a fish. The pontoons of the seaplane slapped the surface of the water, and after a short taxi to the shoreline, the plane came to a shuddering stop. Greg waited for a family of tourists and what appeared to be a couple of business passengers to deplane before standing up and making his way to the exit. He called for an Uber while waiting for his small overnight bag. Friday afternoon traffic in Seattle meant that the short ride to Chrystal's downtown condo would likely take almost as long as the flight from Whisper Island.

When his Uber finally dropped him off, he dialed her unit from the keypad near the front door of the building, and she buzzed him in. When the elevator stopped on her floor, he saw she had left her front door ajar. "Hey, babe," he called, pushing the door open. He could hear the blow dryer running in her primary bathroom, so he made his way to the living room. His gaze took in the monochromatic colors and design. *This room is impersonal and cool,* he noted once again, *with sharp edges like the woman who lives here.*

Taking a seat on the beige leather couch, his gaze was drawn to the oversized framed photograph of Chrystal hanging above her fireplace. The black-and-white photo showed her lying on her stomach in the wet sand, with ocean waves lapping directly behind her. Her lithe, tanned body and skimpy white bikini were each sprinkled by a glittering mix of ocean spray and sand. Propped up on one elbow, her wet blonde hair raked back, and her face tilted so that her eyes looked directly into the camera lens, the effect was stunning.

While he could appreciate the aesthetic of the photo, he wished that Chrystal would replace it with any other piece of art or, better yet, a television. He was reasonably sure that, for her, the photo represented a promising modeling career that had never quite materialized, and that it was ego rather than satisfaction that kept it hanging in prime viewing space.

The hair dryer shut off, and he heard the staccato of her heels on the hallway floor. Greg stood, and Chrystal smiled as she rounded the corner and saw him. She blew him a kiss while backing away from his embrace. "Sorry, babe, my makeup needs to set for a minute," she said. She was dressed in a white silk collared shirt with black leather pants. She had accessorized the look with a matte-toned, silver metallic belt, mirroring the metals of the long, dangling earrings and the choker encircling her elegant neck. Her icy blonde hair was styled in its typical razor-straight bob, and the makeup on her gorgeous face did appear to be dewy.

"You look amazing," Greg said, meaning it even as he knew she expected the compliment.

"Thank you." Her eyes met his briefly and then dropped immediately to his empty hand. "You should have helped yourself to a drink while you waited. What can I get you?"

"Babe, I just got here. I'll have a bourbon neat and thank you." He resumed his seat on the couch and accepted the drink when she handed it to him. He took a sip and felt the satisfying warmth as the liquor trickled down his throat.

"What are your thoughts for the evening?" he asked, taking another sip as Chrystal poured herself a glass of sparkling water, adding a lime twist.

"I thought we could start with drinks at the Tiger Lounge, and then I made reservations for eight at Le Lapin Elegant. Probably hit a club after that."

Greg nodded, keeping his expression neutral. *We don't have anything in common,* he couldn't help thinking. "Sounds good, babe, but let's play the club by ear. I was up early this morning, kayaking before going to the office, so it's been a long day already."

Chrystal's eyes went flat, and her tone turned cool. "You should have planned your morning better. You know I don't do early nights."

He felt his jaw tense, and he matched her coolness with his own. "Maybe you should brush up on the art of compromise?"

Her face immediately softened. Walking over to him, she bent down, winding her arms around his neck, and gave him a long, slow, promising kiss. "You're right, that was very insensitive of me. We can find better things to do tonight. I hope you're not too tired for that?" she purred sexily in an exaggerated breathy tone. But when Greg focused on her green eyes, they were still flat.

An hour later, perched on a stool at the bar of the Tiger Lounge, Greg sipped his bourbon and scrutinized Chrystal with a new awareness. She was in her element, he decided—stunning to look at, expensively dressed, and completely aware of both facts. She held a martini, which Greg was sure she would not finish, and fed off the attention she generated. The bartenders seemed to know her well, and she exchanged generic pleasantries with another couple. But her eyes scanned the room repeatedly to see who was looking back at her. *How have I never noticed how self-absorbed she is?*

Perhaps he was relaxed from the drinks he'd had earlier, or maybe it was the delicious food, but Greg enjoyed dinner. Seated in an intimate booth, the two of them shared an excellent bottle of white Burgundy and chilled oysters, which were both salty and sweet, with a satisfying minerality. Chrystal ordered the salad niçoise, and he decided on the duck, which was exceptional. He even enjoyed the conversation—Chrystal had a cynical yet clever outlook on life, and they shared several laughs. Still, he was pleased when she kept her earlier promise and suggested they head back to her place once they had finished dinner.

When they returned to her condo, Chrystal turned on a few low lights and offered Greg a brandy. She selected music that he recognized as the electronic genre she preferred. He sensed that Chrystal was in seductress mode and kept his face neutral. *This is out of character for her, but I'll follow her lead.*

Putting down her barely tasted glass of champagne, Chrystal stood, reaching for his hand and pulling him to his feet. She led the way to her bedroom. Once inside, she hit a dim light and, wrapping her arms around his neck, kissed him deeply. With her heels on, she was easily six feet tall, and as she pressed her long, sexy body against his, everything between them fit perfectly. Her mouth tasted like champagne and promise.

Backing up a step, she began unbuttoning her silk shirt. She wasn't wearing a bra, and the nipples on her small breasts were erect. He reached for her, but she just smiled and stepped out of his grasp. She removed her leather pants, leaving only the unbuttoned silk shirt and a sexy lace thong, before returning to where he stood.

She pulled him close, rubbing her nipples against him and pressing against his erection. Greg began pulling at the buttons on his shirt. "Here, let me," she said in a husky voice, slowly undoing the buttons and pressing wet, open-mouthed kisses against his chest.

Greg reacted by pulling her roughly to him and kissing her lips hungrily. His hands cupped her breasts greedily, tracing the swollen nipples. She groaned deep in her throat and pulled urgently at his remaining clothing.

Tonight, Chrystal was the aggressor—there was a sense of urgency in her lovemaking that Greg had never seen before. Fully undressed now, she pushed him down onto her bed. She rose over him, and her earrings flashed like fire as they fell forward, against the curve of her cheek. She straddled his body with her own and, in one fluid moment, impaled herself deeply on him. The pleasure was pure and explosive. Together, they found a matching tempo and then release. They lay loosely entwined, each of them silent. *Even when the sex is good, I want to leave,* Greg mused sleepily as he drifted off.

Chapter Seven

Rheagan spent the better part of the week repurposing Mike's office. She gave the existing furniture to Trey in exchange for his assistance in removing it, and she swapped a long, rustic table for one with dark wood grain and black, X-curved metal legs. A coordinating console table against the wall held neat stacks of culinary magazines, standing rows of cookbooks, and several green plants. She decided to leave up the large pegboards for pictures, notes, whatever, and she added a couple of large, framed prints to other walls.

Standing in the newly decorated space she now thought of as the *Inspiration Room*, she waited to feel *inspired*. Instead, surrounded by the pictures and books that had ignited Mike's creative imagination and, consequently, their restaurant, Rheagan felt only panic. The photos of elevated menu items left her empty and blank. *I'm a trained chef, too. If Mike loved these recipes, why don't they resonate with me? Is this a chef's version of writer's block?*

Rheagan sat on one of the new swivel stools and rested her elbows on the table. She knew the restaurant was still thriving, but they'd noticed a drop-off in dinner reservations recently. *Are frequent diners getting bored with our menu?* The current Savor menu sheet was on the table, and her eyes focused on the last item, a special Mike had created for the fall and winter seasons. The dish was halibut served with a soy-shitake mushroom sauce, accompanied by jasmine rice, and garnished with pickled vegetables. She considered replacing the halibut with something else, but it was a mild fish and popular. *Ugh, juggling these decisions feels overwhelming* … 'Resilient,' her dad had always described her that way. She hoped it was true because, while she had survived many challenging issues recently, she hadn't expected to add a crisis of creativity to the list. *Go back to the basics*, she prompted herself. *Think seasonal and see where that leads you.*

Since it was now spring, Rheagan decided to lighten up the dish and take advantage of some locally grown produce. She had noticed the kale on her last trip to the farm. *Maybe some version of kale risotto*, she mused. *Perhaps lighten the halibut preparation by using dry white wine, fresh herbs such as dill and add a squeeze of lemon.* She jotted a few quick notes in her notebook. She wanted a draft outline of a recipe before Joe arrived to discuss it.

Making herself a cup of coffee, she sipped it while glancing at the regular menu items—basic proteins like salmon, chicken, pork, and beef. She would discuss them with Joe, but she was inclined to leave them alone and focus only on the special. *Baby steps, let's see how this goes …*

She heard him in the hall, followed by a quick tap on the door frame. "Come on in, Joe," she called, and he entered carrying his own cup of coffee and a notebook. Rheagan couldn't help but smile at the look of anticipation on his face as he sat on a barstool and his eyes took in the new table and the thriving plants.

"Wow, this looks great, Chef. The room seems so much bigger."

"Thanks. I was going for a space that fosters inspiration." Pushing the menu sheet into the middle of the wooden table so that each of them could see it, Rheagan spoke again. "I'm hoping that refreshing the menu will boost evening reservations. I thought we would focus on the current special, which is the halibut. What do you think of retaining that protein, or have you heard feedback from diners requesting something else?"

"I think the halibut is good because the basics are covered on the regular menu. It sells, as you know." Leaning back in his chair, he inclined his head slightly before reaffirming, "Yeah, I think we should keep it."

Rheagan nodded. "How about we lighten it up? I was thinking of risotto with spring vegetables, maybe kale. Season with white wine and herbs?"

"I like that. What do you think about coating it with panko? Sometimes when we're using inventory for the family meal, the kitchen staff wants a panko crust. It seems to work well."

"Ahh, nice idea," Rheagan agreed. "Let's play around with adding the fresh herbs into the panko." The two of them spent several more minutes debating wine and herb combinations, as well as risotto cooking techniques. They agreed that the next step was to get the new ingredients in-house and begin testing their conceived dish in the kitchen.

After Joe left, Rheagan calmly looked around the *Inspiration Room* with a fledgling sense of accomplishment. She had a long way to go, but she had a new respect for Joe and for herself.

Chapter Eight

Rheagan pulled her white RAV4 into the gravel parking lot at Orcas Farm and headed toward the heated office in the restored rustic barn. She wanted to check out some fresh spring vegetables for the halibut risotto entree. She had been initially thinking of kale, but as much as she loved it, there were always customers who would balk at it without ever trying it. She wanted to avoid the obvious spring vegetables, such as asparagus and peas, and be more creative. She and Joe had finally decided that she should visit the farm and grab whatever looked good to her.

She opened the door, waving at Melissa, the farm office manager, behind her desk. "Hey Melissa, how are you today?"

"Hey Rheagan, always nice to see you. How can I help you today?"

"Just looking to create a new risotto and wanted to see what kind of spring vegetables you might have on hand. I'm looking for inspiration and will probably try a couple of different versions to see which direction we take."

"Got it. Sam's out there somewhere working. Let me text his cell, and he can help you with ideas and selections." As she spoke, Melissa was already texting Sam, the owner of Orcas Farm.

In a few minutes, the door opened, and Sam's lanky form filled the frame. His always-tanned face wore its typical good-natured grin, and his shoulder-length hair was curly from the morning humidity. "Hey Rheagan, what can I do for you?"

"I am looking to be inspired by what is growing now. I want to update a risotto recipe with something maybe unexpected."

Sam laughed as he stood in muddy boots on the rug. "So, no asparagus."

"Exactly." Rheagan smiled back.

"Come with me," he said, opening the door for her and gesturing for her to follow him outside. He walked down a lane bordered by a windbreak of firs and into the field, steaming in the morning sun. "Let me show you where a lot of our early spring produce is coming up."

It was a lovely spring morning, and Rheagan breathed in the fresh air deeply and angled her face to the sun. *It always feels so good after the gloomy drizzle.* Her heart beat a bit faster just thinking about the chance to be creative. They walked through rows of spring onions, asparagus, and peas, and then she saw what she was looking for.

"Ah, I think I just found it," Rheagan exclaimed. "I think I'll play around with chives. I would like to use the whole plant and even incorporate the purple flowers in some way. I could use them for garnish, of course, but maybe also infuse them into oil to finish the dish …"

"Mmm, that does sound like a good choice."

"Not that the farmer wouldn't say that about any of his produce," Rheagan teased.

"Guilty as charged," Sam said, pulling back the narrow green leaves of the plant so Rheagan could get a better look. He showed her several other options, but she remained sold on the idea of the chives. He helped her fill a small bag with the dark green leaves and then placed the delicate blossoms on top. He also filled a small bag with some lacinato kale.

She tried to pay him for it, but he refused. "Save it for when you decide it's what you want and you're back to place a larger order. Better yet, meet me at Jack's pub on Sunday night and you can buy the first round."

Rheagan laughed and nodded. "Deal, first round is on me!" She was still smiling as she backed out of the parking lot, and then she stiffened. *Whoa … It's not a date, right?*

Rheagan drove back to Savor and handed off the produce to Trey before heading over to The Coffee Bean. She needed to talk to Kate before she started spiraling over Sam's invitation. Kate's assistant, Tracy, waved her on toward the back room, where Rheagan found her friend grinding fresh beans and surrounded by big burlap bags of even more beans.

Rheagan smiled at Kate and took an exaggerated sniff of the fresh coffee bean scent permeating the small space. "Do you have a quick moment?

"Sure. What's up?" Kate asked, with a curious smile.

"Kate, I'm probably being an idiot, but I was just at Orcas Farm, grabbing a couple of items there to play around with for a new recipe. Anyway, when I offered to pay, Sam suggested that I buy the first round at Jack's Pub on Sunday … Kate, do you think he thinks of this as a date?"

Kate smiled, pushing her blonde curls out of her face. "And what if it is? Here, let me get you a coffee. I worry about you spending so much time by yourself." She reached around the coffee grinder to pull down two coffee mugs. Then, from a large thermos-style urn in the corner, she poured each of them a cup. They took a seat at a small table.

"But …" Kate added, grimacing now. "If asking you to buy the first round is Sam's way of asking you out for a date, then I need to give him some dating tips. Maybe he is trying to gauge your potential interest. How do you feel?"

"Oh, Kate, I don't think I'm ready. I'm … I mean … It's been forever since I dated, and I still miss Mike. Sam is a great guy, but I just have a lot going on, and I'm not sure I can take any more complications."

"That's fair, sweetie. Of course you miss Mike—it'd be weird if you didn't. But it's okay to make new connections. Sam is a great guy. I mean, I've known him my whole life." Kate squeezed Rheagan's arm across the table. "His situation is complicated, too, you know. Since Mindy left the island after their divorce, he travels back and forth to Seattle to see his daughter. Maybe two great people with complicated lives could enjoy each other's time and not worry about putting a label on it."

"You're right … I'm getting in front of myself, aren't I?" Rheagan said with a laugh. "You and the handsome veterinarian are usually there, right?"

Kate nodded, grinning. "I see what you're doing … safety in numbers, right? Yes, Jeff and I usually go on Sunday nights to hear the music. And Rheagan, I'm glad you'll be there. It's good for you to get out, and it's time, too … You know that, right?"

Rheagan nodded slowly. "I guess I'll see you there. Thanks for the chat," she said, rising and rinsing her cup in the sink. "I don't know what I'd do without such a good friend." She gave Kate a tight hug on her way out of the back room.

Chapter Nine

Sunday afternoon found Rheagan hunched over a stack of paperwork in her office. The restaurant was closed on Sundays and Mondays, but she found it easier to handle some tasks with fewer interruptions. She was about to leave for the day when she just felt like hearing her dad's voice. Hitting the call button on her phone, she smiled when she heard her father on the other end.

"Rheabug! How's my girl?"

She shook her head at the old childhood nickname. No one in the family could remember how the name had originated, but it had most likely been created by her older brother, Jim. Despite acknowledging that it had likely been intended as an insult, the name had stuck. "Hey, Dad, I'm good. I just needed to hear your voice."

"Ah, honey, I love that, but it also tells me something's up. Talk to me. What's going on?"

"It's nothing major, Dad … I'm just trying to put my hands around the creative side of Savor, and I feel stuck. I'm working with Joe, and we're making progress. I guess it just doesn't feel natural, and I don't really know why." She heard her father take a contemplative breath.

"That was Mike's side of the business, right?"

"Yes, but we always talked about the food, and we designed the original menu together. So, I don't know why I feel stuck."

"Are you under any time pressure to make changes right away?"

"No, not really, I mean, reservations have slowed down a little, but who knows why. Joe and I already have a plan to update the special, and we're happy with it. Down the road, we need to start updating mains and creating other specials. Dad, it just feels harder than I thought it would. Why am I struggling creatively in my own restaurant if this is what I always wanted?"

"My advice would be to take a break from that high-end stuff you serve at your restaurant. Go back to your roots. Just play around creatively with something familiar that doesn't feel like pressure. Use that fancy equipment of yours to make one of those crazy pizzas you used to tell me should be added to my menu. You'll find your way."

Rheagan laughed. "Dad, prosciutto is not crazy, but maybe arugula, rosemary, and pistachios were a bridge too far for Tony's Pizza Place."

"Yeah, and I can sleep at night knowing Jimmy will keep my pepperoni pizza legacy intact after I'm gone." His tone turned serious. "Are you good, Rheabug? Do you want to come home?"

"No, Dad, I haven't made up my mind long-term, but for right now I feel like I need to be here …" As she spoke, she fingered the gold key she had found in Mike's office. *No sense in mentioning this to Dad—it would likely seem as strange to him as it does to me. I'll wait until I know more.*

"Honey, I need to hop, I've got a guy coming over to take a look at our refrigeration unit—it's been bonkers lately. Take care of yourself. And make sure you call your mother."

"Dad, thanks for listening. I like your advice. Maybe I'm overthinking this. Love you so much!"

"Love you too, honey. Call your mom!"

Rheagan set the phone down on her desk and pondered her dad's advice. The notion of doing something familiar to shake loose some creativity actually sounded fun. She and her dad had always shared a love of food. Her brother and her mom worked in the business too, but her dad had always called her the true foodie. *Yeah, I like that idea—it can't hurt to try. And yeah, I do need to call Mom, I just don't feel like dealing with her nagging me to return to Connecticut.*

Nudging the gold key with her finger, she considered what to do about it. She still didn't know if the key had even belonged to Mike. When she'd shown Joe the key, he'd immediately recognized it as a key to a safe-deposit box. Taken aback by that information, she had convinced herself it was nothing—likely Mike had found it during the construction, and somehow it had just gotten wedged in his CIA book.

Even so, she had taken the key to her local bank branch office, and when they told her that it was from the Seal Island branch, she was even more convinced that the key had no meaning. She had considered just leaving it with the helpful teller, but some instinct had caused her to put the key back in her purse. Rheagan now regretted that instinct. Her chest felt tight with the familiar but now heightened anxiety. *Why am I getting a bad feeling about this?* She needed to put this silly issue to rest. She looked up the number for the Seal Island branch and hit the green phone icon.

A male voice answered the phone. "Hello, Bank of America, Seal Island branch. Brad speaking, how may I help you?"

"Hi Brad, my name is Rheagan Rossi. I have a key for a safe-deposit box from your branch. I found it in the office of my fiancé, who passed recently. I doubt this key belonged to him, because we live on Whisper Island, but I thought I should check with you." Rheagan could hear the uncertainty in her voice.

After a measured breath followed by a pause, he replied, "Ms. Rossi I am sorry for your loss. We are unable to disclose the existence or contents of a safe-deposit box to anyone other than the legal owner. Might you have documentation to support your status?"

Rheagan looked at her file cabinet as she spoke. "Yes, I have a copy of his death certificate and his will, which names me as the executor of his estate. I also have my ID, of course."

"I see, Ms. Rossi. Unfortunately, we would need a specific court order allowing you access to the box."

"Oh, I forgot to mention," Rheagan apologized. "I also have something called a letters testamentary, signed by the probate judge. Is that what you need?"

"Yes, to provide you access, we will need the death certificate, the letters testamentary, and your ID."

"Brad, can I ask a favor? If I email you copies of the documents now, can you at least tell me if he even has a box at your branch?"

Rheagan heard him sigh before he replied, "I'm sorry, Ms. Rossi, I recognize this is inconvenient, but I am not at liberty to share that information until I can see the documentation and ID you in person."

Rheagan took her own deep breath. "Thank you, Brad, for your help. I hope to get over there tomorrow." She hit the *End* button and logged off her computer. Grabbing the key in her hand, she left her office. *I need to figure out this damn key so I can chill. Ever since I got access to Mike's iPhone, I've been reading too much into everything. By tomorrow at this time, I will be able to put this behind me.*

Back in her apartment, she picked up the purring Mr. Pickles and held him close. "Did I rescue you or did you rescue me, Mr. Pickles? Huh? "she whispered into his fur as she remembered him as the skinny orange cat she used to see when she visited Sea Lion Perch. He'd been friendly yet wary, but soon the two of them had begun sharing her toasted bagels.

Eventually, he'd trusted her to scoop him up, and she'd taken him over to Jeff's veterinary office to see if he had a microchip. Jeff had checked him over, pronouncing him healthy but undernourished and chip-free. The rest was history. Giving Mr. Pickles one more squeeze and another kiss on his furry head, she put him down. He gave a soft meow of protest and began snaking in and out between her feet while she tried to decide what outfit she should wear to meet Sam for their it's-probably-not-a-date at Jack's Pub.

Chapter Ten

Greg could hear the country music as soon as he parked his car, and it made him smile. It wasn't his favorite genre for sure, but it had absolutely been a part of growing up on Whisper Island. When he opened the door, it took a minute for his eyes to adjust to the dim lighting, but then he saw Kate, Jeff, and Sam sitting in their usual corner on the left side of the bar. He stopped in surprise. Rheagan was with them. That was new—he'd never seen her here before, but he was glad she was out. *Maybe I've been imagining that she's looked extra stressed lately* … He took the empty seat beside Jeff and ordered a beer when the bartender came over.

The band was pretty good, and the beers were cold. *This feels right.* Sam and Kate were two of his oldest friends—they had all grown up on this island together. Kate was the first girl he had kissed, and the memory made him smile. His attention strayed to Rheagan, who was at the far end of their group. She and Sam maintained a steady stream of conversation. Clearly, as a farmer and a chef, the two of them had a lot in common, not to mention a business relationship. He saw Rheagan shake her head in laughter at something Sam appeared to be trying to convince her of. *She fits in so well on Whisper Island. I knew that for sure when she took me to Sea Lion Perch for our latest coffee catch-up.*

Tonight, she was dressed in a white button-down shirt, snug jeans, and boots. She usually wore her long auburn hair up, but tonight it was down, spilling full and loose over her shoulders. She tapped her foot to the rhythm of the music and seemed unaware of how pretty she was. *She's not stuck on herself.* He leaned forward in his seat and, looking over at her, he raised his pint in a toast. She smiled with those damn dimples and raised her wine glass back at him.

Seeing Rheagan in this social setting made him miss Mike even more. Despite not growing up together, the two had formed a strong bond of brotherhood. Both of them had been serious students at the University of Washington. Greg's motivation was to learn the law, step into his father's role in the family law firm and assume a leadership position on the island. Additionally, he'd been groomed to manage the family philanthropic trusts inherited from his mother's family. Mike, on the other hand, had been driven to be a self-made success. Without a family to depend on, he was betting on himself, and he'd seemed to thrive on the pressure.

He and Mike had maintained their bond even once Greg left for law school and Mike abandoned political science to attend culinary school. He was surprised but happy when Mike later decided not only to follow him to Whisper Island but also to put his culinary skills to the test.

Greg paused now, remembering that his friend, Mike, wasn't much of a joiner and was absolutely not a country music fan. *There's no way he would have come here tonight.* Greg took another look toward the end of the bar and decided that Rheagan, on the other hand, seemed to fit in perfectly.

Chapter Eleven

Rheagan was dressed and ready to leave for Seal Island by 11:00 a.m. She had truly enjoyed her evening at Jack's Pub and had decided to make it a regular habit. But today's task still weighed on her mind. The watery sunlight shining into her living room windows lifted her spirits, reminding her that spring was here. Spring in the Northwest was noticeably cooler than in the East Coast shore town she'd grown up in, but she loved all the bursts of color from the sprouting foliage. Everything felt new and fresh.

She decided to walk onto the ferry rather than go through the hassle of taking her RAV4. The harbor and ferry terminal were a short walk from her apartment on Whisper Island, and the Bank of America branch would be a short walk from the ferry terminal on Seal Island. In the light of day, she felt more confident that today's errand was nothing more than an inconvenience. And a good excuse to take some time off and enjoy the scenery along the way.

From the deck of the inter-island ferry, Rheagan gazed across the choppy water as Seal Island neared. She drained the last of her coffee and waited to disembark, with seagulls calling and circling overhead. There were just a handful of other people on the ferry, and Rheagan was quickly on the main street, where she could see the sign for the Bank of America ahead and on her right.

As she opened the bank branch's front door, a young man seated at a table in a small cubicle stood up to greet her with a polite smile.

"Brad?" she questioned, smiling back at him.

"Yes, and you must be Ms. Rossi."

"Rheagan, please—yes. Thanks again for your help yesterday. I've brought the documents you asked for." She felt a stab of anxiety, and her hands shook as she reached into her large shoulder bag to retrieve her files.

"Please sit down, Rheagan." Brad gestured to the chair across from his desk, and she sat, trying to compose herself while he reviewed the papers she had handed him. He began typing on his keyboard.

Rheagan knew before Brad said a word. There was a subtle increase in the stillness of his body as he read the screen in front of him. She felt a wave of sorrow and forced herself to meet his eyes, knowing that her inner turmoil must be visible.

"Rheagan, we do have an account here under the name of Michael Carlucci." Brad's tone was professional, but he spoke more softly, as if he was concerned and maybe even regretful of the information he had to share. "I'll escort you to the vault where we maintain the boxes. After we retrieve it, I can show you to a private area where you can review the contents. Do you need a moment, or would you like to come with me now?"

Rheagan nodded without speaking and stood to follow him. Later, she wouldn't remember going into the vault with Brad or the dual key process they used to retrieve the box. Her mind was too busy trying to rationalize the situation. *There is an explanation, and I will know it soon. Seal Island is primarily agricultural with a tiny population. Perhaps it's related to a supplier for Savor? Right? Except I handle procurement and ordering...*

Alone in the private room, Rheagan sat still, looking at the box. It wasn't large, but whatever Mike had kept here, he hadn't wanted her to know about it. Taking a deep breath, she opened it. The box contained a single, yellowed envelope and a cell phone. Rheagan picked up the cell phone with dread. She hit the power button, knowing that it probably wouldn't work, and it didn't. But even without turning it on, she knew it was the phone he had told her had been lost. With a shaking hand, she removed the envelope and set it on the desk. After a moment, she picked it up and looked at the back side—there was no handwriting on either side. Rheagan inhaled deeply and opened it wide enough to see what appeared to be photos.

Carefully, she pulled them out. There were two, dog-eared and worn like the envelope they had been stored in. There was also an equally worn ticket stub from a Minnesota Twins game. Maybe they had all been pulled from a scrapbook? She turned her attention to the photos. Both included a young girl, possibly a teenager. She was quite simply beautiful, with long black hair and dark eyes. Her hair and outfit evoked the 1990s, perhaps? In one photo, the girl was with a man—his hair dark and wavy—but his face was partially turned away, and he was looking down. The second photo had been taken in front of a commercial building, possibly a restaurant, with a 'Grand Opening' banner hanging from the awning. The girl stood in the arms of what appeared to be the same twenty-something man. In this picture, he had the same tousled, dark, wavy hair, but now you could see his handsome face and confident smile. The girl's deep brown eyes were filled with mischief as she seemed to be pulling back her T-shirt to emphasize a subtly rounded stomach, her glossy lips pursed up in a smug smile.

Rheagan closed her eyes. *So, I wasn't crazy for feeling like Mike wasn't telling me everything. I still don't understand, and I can't just keep blocking these feelings like I've done for so long. Mike, what does any of this mean?* She took one deep, steadying breath and returned the items to the envelope. She pressed the button on the wall and waited for Brad.

In a blur, she completed the paperwork to close the safe-deposit box account. She thought to request a log history for the account, which Brad included along with the other paperwork. Rheagan thanked him for his time and retraced her steps to the ferry, welcoming the salty breeze after the stuffy bank interior. While she waited for the next boat, she reviewed the log with a shaking hand. The log showed that Mike had established the account two days after they had moved to Whisper Island. In addition, he had accessed the box on June 16 of that same year and the following year, with the last time being July 2, just two weeks later. Rheagan tucked the log back into the file and took another deep breath. *I can't do this on my own anymore.* She dialed Greg's cell phone. It was time to involve him in this—maybe he would have some answers.

She heard the call go straight to voicemail and squared her shoulders. "Greg, this is Rheagan. I found something of Mike's that I don't understand. Maybe there's been more… I mean, maybe you know something, too? Do you have time to drop by tonight around seven? I'll make us a bite. I know it's last-minute, so thank you. Umm, just let me know …" When she hit the *End* button, she felt a sense of relief.

Chapter Twelve

Greg glanced at his phone and saw he was ten minutes earlier than she'd said. He buzzed the security entrance to Rheagan's private upstairs space—he was anxious to see her. Her earlier message had concerned him, but when he'd tried to call her back, her phone had gone straight to voicemail. He pushed the entrance open when she released the lock. As he reached the top of the stairs, he could already smell the delicious aroma of a home-cooked meal. He sniffed appreciatively—*garlic for sure, maybe meatballs?* He acknowledged his sadness that Mike wouldn't be there.

At his knock, she called for him to enter, and met him in the entryway, enveloping him in a hug that was tighter than usual. He looked into her striking caramel eyes and noted the purple shadows beneath them. He had brought her six white roses because they just looked like her, understated but elegant. He had noticed that about her, even when casually dressed, she somehow always had style. Tonight, she was wearing a simple cream sweater and jeans; her long hair was pulled back in a messy bun that looked both effortless and chic. He handed the flowers to her, noticing her eyes light up when she leaned in to smell their delicate scent.

"Greg, thank you for coming over and for the roses, too." Rheagan's smile finally reached her eyes. "Let me just put these in some water and get you a glass of wine."

He followed her to the kitchen, where she laid the roses on the counter and reached for a wine glass. Greg leaned forward and took her hand, squeezing it before releasing it. "Rheagan, I'm glad you called me. You sounded upset, and then I couldn't reach you by phone. Are you okay?"

He heard her inhale deeply, but she only nodded as she poured him a glass of Chianti. "I'm okay. I need to talk some things through with you, but …" She put her hand on his arm, and her beseeching eyes caught his own. "Can I please just enjoy your company, and can we share dinner first? To be honest, I need some wine, and my questions will still be here when we are done. Greg, I feel better just having you here."

Greg held her gaze and nodded. "Of course." He would give her time to decompress, if she needed that, but he wasn't leaving until she shared what had upset her. Trying to tamp down his impatience, he took a sip of his wine, allowing himself to appreciate the dryness on his tongue, and watched as she deftly trimmed the stems of the roses and arranged the flowers in a clear glass vase. The kitchen timer beeped, and Rheagan moved to check a pot on the stove. Joining her there, he peered into the pot. "I was hoping I smelled meatballs," he said with an anticipatory grin.

Rheagan smiled back at him. "My dad's famous recipe with a few of my own creative touches." She filled a large pot with water to boil the pasta. "Why don't you open another bottle of wine and take the salad to the dinner table?" She squeezed his arm. "Greg, thank you again for being here."

He placed the decanted bottle of wine and the caprese salad on Rheagan's dining room table and took a moment to appreciate the warmth and style of her home. Greg had seen enough of Mike's apartments over the years to be certain that this was all Rheagan's doing. The colors were neutrals—creams and tans—with splashes of marigold. Warm woods, mixed with dark metals, and neutral fabrics with diverse textures and weaves, created an interesting, layered look throughout the space. The walls held oversized, colorful, and eclectic art. It was a space as welcoming as Rheagan herself—her home invited you to stay and unwind. He conjured up an image of Chrystal's stylish condo, realizing that in comparison, Chrystal's home served solely as a stylish wrapper for the attractive woman who lived there.

He shook off his musing and returned to the kitchen to find Rheagan plating two pasta bowls with spaghetti. She topped each bowl with meatballs and poured the aromatic red sauce over them.

"Here, let me," he offered, and she handed the dishes off to him, reaching for a hunk of Parmesan and a small hand grater and following him to the dining area.

The salad was delicious—trust a chef to select the freshest tomatoes and basil. However, the meatballs made him groan out loud in appreciation. "These meatballs are so good. I can't believe they aren't on your menu."

"Mike designed Savor's menus as fine dining, so I'm not sure the Rossi family meatballs meet that high standard. This is the food I grew up with and still make for my friends and myself." Her expression turned sheepish, "I was talking to my dad the other day about feeling creatively blocked while updating the menu for downstairs. He suggested that I ease up and play around with familiar recipes. So here we are."

Greg lifted his wine glass in a toast, "Here's to practice, and I'm available whenever you want company."

Rheagan smiled at him before asking, "Did I interrupt any important city council work tonight?"

"No, our regular meeting is tomorrow night, where I am sure we will pick up again with the heated discussions about Airbnb popularity. The resort and the traditional B&Bs are opposed to the homeowners getting into their space."

"I get it … I grew up in a shore town on the other side of the country, and competition for tourists and their money is fierce."

Greg nodded, appreciating how much the two of them had in common. While Rheagan had wanted to leave the small town where she had grown up, Greg had known he would never leave Whisper Island. He had witnessed his father help shape this community, and he had always wanted to play a similar role. He also appreciated the beauty and the laid-back lifestyle it provided. College and law school had drawn him away, but now that he was back, it felt right to be here.

Rheagan spoke again, interrupting his train of thought. "The Connecticut shore has been booming with tourists for years. I think they've tried to balance things out by requiring Airbnb hosts to have a business license and a minimum rental period of one month. That kept the overnight and weekend revenues with the traditional retail models and helped to keep out folks just looking for a weekend party house to rent."

Greg nodded again. "Thanks, Rheagan, that's an interesting solution I can bring to our discussions." He paused. "Does it bother you that you left one shore town only to end up in another?"

She laughed lightly. "No, they feel entirely different. Growing up, the tourists were really only a summer thing, but it felt like they took over the town. I hated it—even as I knew that most of the residents, like my own parents, depended on the revenues all those visitors created. Because the seasons are more moderate here and we are a considerable distance from Seattle, tourists seem more evenly distributed throughout the year. And most importantly, the ratio here is always more residents than tourists."

Greg nodded. "I get that." He took another bite of his meatball. "So, what did you add to the Rossi family recipe?" he asked, realizing that even though delaying their conversation about Mike hadn't been his idea, he was appreciating the chance to take a breath and enjoy the food and Rheagan's company.

"My dad adds a little bit of sugar to offset the acidity of the tomatoes. Instead, I sautéed carrots along with the onion and garlic to achieve the same result. I also added some minced anchovies that melt into the sauce, so you don't even know they're there, but they add depth and complexity. Lastly, I couldn't help myself… There's a lot more spice in my meatballs and sauce. By the way, I made extra so that I will be sending you home with leftovers."

Greg smiled widely and took another bite. "So, what was it like growing up in the restaurant business?"

"Ha," Rheagan paused, her brow furrowed as she thought about the question. "It was hectic, frustrating, and wonderful, and often all at once. It's a family business, so there was a lot of arguing. As a child, it was magical—the restaurant was my playground. As a teenager, I still loved it, but I felt like I was performing unpaid labor, and often wanted to escape and spend time with my friends. As an adult, it was bittersweet: I loved it deeply, but I knew I couldn't thrive in that town and at that family restaurant. I wanted to make my own food."

"So, is that what you're doing now? Making your own food?" Greg's perceptive eyes held her gaze.

"I don't know …" Rheagan said softly. "Maybe I need to think about that."

"Rheagan, Savor is all yours now. You should follow your passion even if it means deviating from the original vision you and Mike shared."

She nodded slowly, but her eyes looked uncertain as she stood to clear the table. Greg stood too, helping her carry dishes to the kitchen. He was glad he had shared that observation with Rheagan. She was so talented, and Savor should feel like hers. *I want her to be happy here. She was always Mike's girl to me, but now she's just Rheagan, and I'm enjoying getting to know her better. I really don't want her to leave Whisper Island.*

Chapter Thirteen

Greg insisted on helping with the cleanup, and with both of them, the work went quickly. Rheagan handed off the half-full wine bottle and their glasses, then followed him to the living room, carrying a cheese and fruit platter.

"Do you mind if I let my cat, Mr. Pickles, out to join us?"

Greg smiled. "Of course not. Jeff was telling me about the little guy last night."

A moment later, he heard the light pounding of energetic paws, and Mr. Pickles made his entrance. His curious green gaze focused on Greg, and he immediately headed in his direction, accepting a scratch under his chin before settling down in his cat bed, seemingly content to be near Rheagan.

As soon as Rheagan was seated, Greg focused all his attention on the woman beside him. "Okay, Rheagan, talk to me. Your message said that you had found something of Mike's."

She sighed heavily and met his eyes. "I feel like I need to give you some background …" Her voice quivered slightly, and she took a small sip of her wine before continuing. Greg reached for her hand, trying to impart strength and comfort through his touch.

"After Mike's death, I cleaned out his belongings from our home. Greg, I didn't find anything personal—nothing. Not a note or a card from me, from you, from anyone. It made me sad, and to be honest, it made me uncomfortable."

"I'm sorry, I don't know what to say ..." Greg reached for the wine bottle and topped off their glasses. "You were right to call me, Rheagan. Mike was important to both of us. He was, as you know, very private and self-contained, but still, I'm surprised ... That seems almost sterile."

He heard her take a deep breath.

"There's more," she said softly. "So, I found a key in his office, and long story short, I discovered he had a safe-deposit box on Seal Island."

"What the hell!" Greg interrupted, his expression worried and questioning.

"I found his old cell phone in the safe-deposit box. I don't remember exactly when, maybe two or three months before he died, Mike told me he had lost his phone. He bought a new one, and you probably remember that he got a Washington phone number to replace the California number that he had from our culinary school days. Well, after the delays with the probate process, I recently gained access to the data on his replacement phone, and, Greg, it was just like our house ... There were no pictures, no texts, nothing personal on that phone at all. Greg, you and I are not even in his contacts."

"What the fuck!? He was deleting every message and text as he got them from us?"

Rheagan got up from the sofa and retrieved an envelope from the counter. When she returned, she opened the envelope and handed him the two pictures, the ticket stub, and the log history. "He was keeping these items there, too. He made annual visits to see them on June 16th. He went there again in July of this year, but I think that coincided with him supposedly losing his phone. Greg, I don't understand what any of this means."

Greg turned his attention to the pictures, turning them over as Rheagan had done. He made no effort to mask his confusion.

"What do you know about his mother?" Rheagan's voice interrupted his growing frustration.

"Do you think this is his mother? He didn't talk about her. I assumed that it was too painful because of losing her to cancer. Say this is her—maybe she's even pregnant with him. Why would two old pictures of his mother, possibly his father, and a baseball ticket stub be the only personal items he kept? And why would he lie about losing his phone and then take it to Seal Island? Why these items, and why the hell did he need to keep them in a safe-deposit box on another fucking island?" Greg realized he had raised his voice and forced himself to take a deep breath. He turned to face Rheagan; her eyes were haunted. Greg hated that he had no answers to wipe the hurt and the fear from her beautiful face.

Mr. Pickles jumped onto the sofa and curled up in Rheagan's lap. *My yelling scared him*, Greg acknowledged with a degree of guilt, as Rheagan gathered the cat close to her. Lost in his thoughts, he idly traced the bottom photo and the ticket stub with his finger. "Wait a minute, look at the date on this ticket. It's dated June 16th, which corresponds with his visits per the log. And look at the year. Mike would have been what, about ten years old if this was his ticket?"

Rheagan's face wore a puzzled expression. "I hadn't noticed that … Are the visits about the baseball game, the girl, or are they somehow connected? I know he loved baseball, but he never mentioned the Twins to me."

Greg shook his head. "Mike loved the sport, but as much as we discussed it, he never mentioned the Twins more than in passing. Rheagan, I'm sorry I don't have the answers you were probably hoping for. This leaves me feeling like I didn't know him as well as I thought I did." He turned on the couch to face her and reached out, putting his hands lightly on her shoulders to turn her toward him so he could see her face.

"It's okay, Greg, I'm just thankful not to be handling all this on my own." Her eyes began to water, and Greg wiped a tear away with the pad of his thumb.

"We will figure this out together." Greg reached for their wine glasses and handed Rheagan hers.

"Thanks, Greg, you don't know how much it means to me." Rheagan smiled a bit. "And you were Mike's best friend—that's not up for debate. Remember that time you guys did a polar plunge?"

Greg laughed and almost choked on his wine. "Rheagan, give a guy some warning." She giggled in response, and then they shared more memories of good times with Mike.

"Wow, it's gotten late. I should probably head home and let you get your rest. You're back to work tomorrow, right?" Greg stood, reaching for the empty bottle and their wine glasses. He headed toward the kitchen, and Rheagan followed with the remainder of the cheese tray and plates.

At her front door, Greg held her tight and left her with a kiss on her forehead and a promise to be in touch. Much later, along with all the questions Mike had left behind for them, the scent of Rheagan's perfume and those damn dimples lingered on his mind.

Chapter Fourteen

The next morning, as she drove to the local supermarket, Rheagan could feel the difference in her attitude. She knew Greg as a loyal friend, a problem solver, and someone who kept his emotions in check. His intense reactions to the information she had shared the night before validated her feelings. She was glad she had invited him over. It had felt so good to unload her concerns and questions. She allowed herself a slight pang of sadness for the one secret she had kept for herself. Determined to have a good day anyway, she pushed the sadness away—she had become quite skilled at compartmentalizing.

While browsing for the daily restaurant provisions, she thought about how satisfying it had felt to make dinner for Greg. Working with her old recipes and flavors had felt so natural and fun. Her dad's advice had been spot-on, and she felt inspired to try another dish. *Why not make my special pizza for the family meal at Savor tonight? I can give the guys a break from cooking and save myself from having a freezer full of leftover pizza at home.* With a smile, she added pistachios to her shopping basket.

She was still smiling as she pulled her car to the rear of Savor to unload. Manny was outside, watering the potted herbs with Rheagan's neon-pink watering can. The whole crew had been excited about trying some new flavor combinations, but none more than Manny. He set the watering can down and hurried to the back door to help with the produce.

"Chef," he said as his muscular arms reached around her to grab the heavier-looking bags. "I was talking to Charlie, who just opened that bottle shop down the block." While he spoke, he nudged the back door to Savor open. They entered, laying their bags near the stainless-steel counter, which served as their sorting table. "Anyway, he noticed our herb pots, and he's interested in doing a cross promotion with you featuring his alcohol and your fresh herbs and fabulous food."

"Ah, that's an interesting idea. I do love muddled basil in my gin on the rocks. Thanks, Manny, I'll reach out to him." The idea appealed to her—she liked the community element of the two businesses working together, and she had always wanted Savor to have a bar presence. Mike had not been a drinker, and while he recognized that a successful restaurant needed to serve alcohol, he strongly opposed a bar with seating. They had compromised on making drinks in the back and serving them to the tables. *Changing the bar setup hasn't even crossed my mind, but maybe it's another way for me to feel creative here.*

Rheagan left Joe and the rest of the team to put away the produce and headed to her office to place orders, pay bills, and handle the endless other tasks required to manage a restaurant and staff. She also called Charlie, and they set up a time for him to drop by with various spirits. He was especially excited to work with the lavender she was growing. Rheagan hung up the phone and brewed herself some coffee. She took her mug into the *Inspiration Room* and sat at the table, gazing at the greenery, sipping her coffee and acknowledging that she was beginning to feel more comfortable in her solo role at Savor.

As she stood to return to her office, her eyes caught sight of Mike's CIA study manual. She had kept it because she couldn't bear to get rid of it. But now, it occurred to her that she had found the safe-deposit key in that book. *Does this book hold any other secrets from Mike?* She took the book back to the table and leafed slowly through every page, finding nothing else tucked in the pages. Mike's handwritten notes ripped painfully at her heart, but they referenced only cooking techniques and flavor combinations. With a sigh, she closed the manual and replaced it on the shelf.

She had told Joe that she had a surprise for the team and that she'd be handling the family dinner tonight. It was a regular practice in the restaurant business for various kitchen staff members to take turns creating a meal to be shared by all scheduled staff, both front-of-house and back-of-house. The dinner was served each day before the restaurant opened to its evening guests. At Savor, the meal was generally a raucous and often competitive occasion, but always a good bonding experience, and she couldn't wait to try out her idea.

Rheagan took a quick tour of the kitchen and dining room before starting her prep. She did this every day to ensure that the restaurant was well-positioned for a successful dinner service. Nodding her head in approval, she made her way to the kitchen and began laying out the ingredients to make her pizzas. She had prepared the dough earlier and taken it out of the refrigerator as soon as she'd come downstairs, allowing it to reach room temperature. She planned to make three different kinds of pizzas: a pepperoni with her version of hot honey, a margherita for the vegetarians on the staff, and her personal favorite, the white pizza with prosciutto and arugula. As she began preparing the red sauce that would serve as the base for the pepperoni and margherita, Joe, Manny, and Trey came over to inspect her ingredients.

"Mise en place, folks. Note how neat Chef's work area is; we can all learn from her," Joe said with a snicker. It was a running joke with the cooking team that Rheagan was obsessively neat and organized. She joined in laughing along with the others. It was true—she owned it.

"I can't lie, I'm pretty psyched about this," Manny said. "There is no good Italian food on this island. With last names like both Mike's and yours, I expected legit Italian food when you guys moved here and began working on your restaurant."

Rheagan paused. "I never thought of it, but you're right. The resort offers a token pasta option, and there's a Domino's pizza, but that's it, isn't it? I cook Italian at home, so I never think about going out for it." The men returned to their tasks, and she resumed her prep, but now she felt expectant, like this might just be the beginning of something.

When it was ready, Rheagan began tossing the dough in the air, letting it stretch and form air pockets that would create a lighter, crispier crust. All three men returned and took their turns with varying success. "It takes practice," Rheagan said, laughing at Manny's frustrated face.

To compensate for not having the screaming-hot pizza oven she had grown up with in her family's restaurant, she cobbled together a solution using a pizza stone from her upstairs apartment and some good, old cast-iron pans from the restaurant. The smell of melted cheese, garlic, and toasty crust acted like a magnet, drawing the team to the table for dinner.

She smiled as they jostled each other to reach for their favorite slice. Taking a bite of her favorite pizza, she savored the crunch of toasted pistachios and peppery arugula, paired with savory prosciutto and hints of garlic and rosemary.

As was their usual practice, the conversation turned to analyzing the ingredients and techniques. "Chef, I love that prosciutto pizza. I've never had a bunch of those flavors on a pizza before. What other creative pizzas have you made?" Manny's expression was intense, and Rheagan recognized again that of her staff, he was the most curious about new tastes and textures.

"Honestly, I think of pizza as a blank canvas that can take on anything. One of my favorites is another white pizza with garlic, basil, prosciutto or bacon, and eggs with the white set but the yolk still runny."

"Oh man, that sounds good. I need to think about this." Manny took another bite of his pizza. "It's like how I felt when you showed us that pesto can be so many combinations besides basil and pine nuts."

Joe intentionally jostled Manny while reaching for another slice of the pepperoni pizza. "Better get your head out of your creative cloud—we've got a busy night ahead." Laughter erupted around the table, and Manny grinned, nodding good-naturedly at his sous chef.

The meal was wrapping up, and the dishwashers started clearing the table. Rheagan headed into the dining room to review the evening's schedule. Joe found her there and tapped her on the shoulder. She turned with a questioning smile. "What can I do for you, Joe?"

"Chef, I just wanted to say that it was fun watching you in the kitchen tonight, making the meal. I know you grew up in a pizza restaurant, and this pizza lived up to that—it was delicious. It felt like you were cooking the food you love."

"Thanks, Joe." As Joe headed back toward the kitchen, her mind turned over his comments. Savor's business phone rang suddenly, jolting her attention back to the evening ahead.

After a busy dinner shift, closing the restaurant, and saying goodbye to Joe, Rheagan headed upstairs and kicked her shoes off in her entryway. She carried them into the bedroom to put them in their designated space in her overly organized closet. "My feet are killing me tonight, and I have you to thank for that," she said aloud, looking balefully at the shiny black pumps.

Mr. Pickles wandered into her closet and began winding around her feet as she changed from her front-of-the-house clothes into her pajamas. Bending down, she scooped him up and pressed kisses on his head while she carried him into the kitchen. When she put him down to pour herself a glass of wine, he meowed in objection and resumed his winding while she tossed some baguettes to toast in the oven and sliced a wedge of brie. A few minutes later, with her evening snack laid out on the island, she scooped up Mr. Pickles and sat down to unwind.

Today was a good day. But it was more than just that. She was feeling a new engagement with Savor. Taking a sip of her wine, she began organizing her thoughts around the restaurant. What were the sources of the energy and excitement that she was feeling? Some of that came from renewed confidence—the recognition that she could run the restaurant single-handedly. But the real energy and excitement seemed to be about envisioning changes to Savor that felt more intrinsic to her. Plus, she had received what felt like positive feedback from two people, in addition to her dad, whose opinions mattered most to her. Greg had advised that she should make Savor her own. And Joe, who knew her cooking, had recognized that today's meal had been about authenticity, not just technique. *But wait, it's more than that—I feel more engaged with myself. Today, I made the effort to style my hair in the "hot girl" ponytail, and I wore those damn pumps ...*

She allowed herself to bask in the optimism before acknowledging the guilt. She had loved Mike, and his loss was an enduring ache. However, she needed to be honest with herself—their perfect future had been showing signs of strain.

When she had taken Mike to Connecticut to meet her folks, their visit had lacked the easy warmth and camaraderie that she had expected. Despite their shared experience managing restaurants, the conversation between her family and Mike had seemed superficial and strained. When she had tried to talk to him about it, he had seemed sad that she was disappointed, but oddly unremorseful, which had hurt her deeply.

A few days later, she'd brought the issue up again. In an uncharacteristically vulnerable revelation, he admitted to struggling with building meaningful relationships with people. This wasn't a complete surprise, since she had seen it herself at times, even with their own staff. But she was surprised by Mike's reluctance to work on that. Still, having seen his vulnerability, she felt protective of him.

Maybe because she loved Mike and felt that new sense of protectiveness, she had given in to him too much. His energy and appetite for experiencing life often led him to make decisions for both of them, usually leaving her to clean up the details when he lost interest. She was starting to realize that even with Savor, she had allowed too much of Mike's vision to dictate the food and menu, and with him gone, she had struggled to feel her own connection. *But that is changing. I know now that I want to stay on Whisper Island, and I need to make Savor my own. I love you, Mike. I'll never know what the future would have held for us, but I miss you, and it doesn't feel fair for you not to be here … I don't understand what I've recently discovered, so I can't move forward without doing this one last thing to understand you better.*

Rheagan smeared some creamy brie on her warm baguette and took a bite, focusing on the crunch and the buttery, rich flavor. She knew Mike had grown up nearby in the city of SeaTac. She would pull together a plan and take a quick trip. *Maybe I can find some answers there.*

Chapter Fifteen

Kate leaned back on Rheagan's couch, idly petting Mr. Pickles, who was sitting on her lap. She reached around him to grab her wine glass and took a sip. "Ahh, I like this … What is this wine?"

"It's a Sancerre, from the Loire Valley. I like it too. Can I give you a bottle to take home?"

"Oh god no, I would drink it, and mornings come early for a coffee shop owner." Kate grimaced comically, making Rheagan laugh. "So, spill, girl. How did it go with Sam? Did you feel any sparks? Do you think he did?"

Rheagan tipped her head in a quizzical pose. "I didn't on my end, and I don't really think so on his end, either. He talked a lot about Mindy and their daughter, Amy. I guess that if he were interested in me romantically, he would have mentioned her less or at least in less positive ways. He left me with the impression that he is sad she took off, but proud of her and still hopeful that things may work out."

Kate's expression turned thoughtful. "When you grow up in a small place like Whisper Island, there are the kids who love it and know that they will stay, and then there are those who can't wait to leave. Mindy was always in the camp that wanted to leave. She often said she wanted to experience more of life, and she hated that in a small town, everyone knew your business. Poor girl, she experienced that the hard way when she and Sam got pregnant."

"Had they dated a long time?" Rheagan asked, sipping her wine.

"They had been on and off for a long time. The offs were probably because she wanted to leave, but Sam was always going to inherit the family farm. I'm not even sure that they were technically dating when she got pregnant, but they married anyway and had Amy." Kate waved her wine glass in the air. "Now Mindy's in Seattle, working for a law firm. Sounds like Sam is hoping that she'll get the wanderlust out of her system. I told you it was complicated … They both dote on Amy."

"Yeah, it does sound complicated." Rheagan shrugged. "But he told me that the two of them still get along really well and co-parent well, too. He told me that he actually stays at Mindy's apartment when he visits them."

"Okaaay, that sounds even more complicated than I thought." Kate scrunched her nose. "I'm glad you didn't feel sparks. Interestingly enough, I notice that Greg looks at you an awful lot. Any sparks there?"

Rheagan laughed. "What kind of a friend are you? Greg has a girlfriend, a model, I might add."

Kate laughed too. "That will never last—they never do with him. You should know that. He's been through a few girlfriends just since you've been on the island. He's looking for something else—I just don't think he knows it yet. And hear me out, Rheagan, Greg acts differently with you."

"I don't know … We just have a common link to Mike."

Kate shook her head. "Don't get mad at me for saying this, but as an observer, I think you and Greg have a more natural and chemical connection than the one I sensed between you and Mike."

Rheagan reached for Kate's hand. "I always want you to speak your mind. Mike was hard sometimes, and we had our struggles. We were working through it ..."

Kate squeezed the hand Rheagan held. "I'm sorry to hear that, and I'm sure it makes his loss harder. Just keep an open mind on what you and Greg are building. Perhaps it stems from having his last name etched on hospitals and schools, but Greg has always had a tough time trusting women. He definitely enjoys your company—and spends a lot of time with you. 'Coffee Catch-ups,'" Kate said, acting out the air quotes.

"Oh, come on!" Rheagan thumped Kate with a throw pillow, and they ended the evening laughing.

Chapter Sixteen

Greg paused on the sidewalk and turned his full attention to Rheagan. "I don't like the idea of you doing this on your own." He reached out to touch her arm, and she stopped for a moment, too. Her gaze met his, and he saw the determination in her eyes and the stubborn set of her chin. "Can you wait until I'm available to join you?"

Rheagan gave him that smile that didn't reach her eyes and shook her head, slowly. "I don't know if anything will come of this trip, but it's where I need to start. I really want some answers, Greg." She began walking again down the tree-lined street.

He sighed and took a small sip of his coffee. They were out for their regularly scheduled coffee walk, and Rheagan had surprised him by bringing up her idea to travel to SeaTac on Monday. "Can we review your plan? Maybe I can help." Her eyes brightened, and her dimples flashed. *It's hard to refuse this girl.*

"First of all, I know this is a long shot, and it might be a waste of my time, but I have to try … I tried to determine the high school he graduated from by searching online. I couldn't find any definitive information, but the city of SeaTac is small, with only one high school, so I plan to start there. I'm going to bring my ID and probate documents, and I'll see if I can find someone who knew him, like a teacher or coach."

"Hmm … even with your probate docs, they may be reluctant to share any information. Schools have very tough privacy rules. At the very least, you could ask for yearbooks and see if you find his picture in them. But," he reached out to touch her arm again, "you could end up getting shut down."

"Oh, good idea, on the yearbooks. And Greg, I know … But I need to do *something*."

"All right, what else are you thinking?"

"I'm hoping they will share his old address, and I can drive by and see if there are neighbors."

"That's a long shot. They really shouldn't give you that information. So, tell me what you think you might learn by talking to people who knew him?" Greg held her gaze, hoping to convey his concern.

"Greg, I don't understand why he kept secrets from us. Maybe the answer will come from learning more about his past. I want to see if those pictures were of his mother." The serious expression on her face unnerved him.

"Rheagan, please, are you sure you can't wait for me to join you?"

"Greg, we both know this is a long shot … I am more likely to get information on my own as the sympathetic fiancée."

He gave a reluctant nod. "Please keep your cell phone on and keep me posted." He looked intently into her eyes, waiting for her answer.

Rheagan nodded, but her eyes looked troubled.

Back at his office, Greg pushed his leather chair away from his very cluttered desk. He stretched his arms over his head, trying to alleviate the pain in the back of his neck. Too much online research today. He wondered, not for the first time, whether it might make sense to hire a paralegal to support his practice. The downside of being a small-town lawyer was that you had to be a jack of all trades, and that increased the time spent on new areas of the law.

Nan poked her head into his office to ask if he wanted a cup of coffee, and he smiled gratefully and gave her a thumbs-up as his cellphone began to ring. Chrystal's name flashed on the display, and his hand paused for a moment before he picked it up.

"Hey, babe," he answered, recognizing the distraction in his voice.

"You must be busy …" The petulance in her tone told him she had noticed it, too. "I want to come see you this weekend. It's been a couple of weeks, and I thought my going your direction would be a nice change."

Greg didn't have a good excuse on hand and felt a sense of inevitability. Against his better judgment, he countered, "I have a new case that needs some research."

"That's fine, I'll come Saturday afternoon and leave on Monday morning. That will give you Saturday morning to get some work done."

He bit back a sigh. "That works. Let me help with your travel plans, and I'll pick you up."

"Great, babe, talk soon."

He heard her end the call using what he always viewed as her contrived breathy voice, and he gave vent to a full-throated sigh. He was frustrated with himself—he needed to talk to her. The relationship wasn't working for him, and he had been putting off the discussion they needed to have. Now it would only be worse because they would be on his turf, and he wouldn't be able to control his escape. He sighed again before turning back to his research.

Chapter Seventeen

Chrystal set her phone down with a speculative look on her face. Greg had not wanted her to join him this weekend. She preferred that his reluctance be business-related and not personal, but honestly, either reason required a plan. She scolded herself for letting things get this far. They had been talking less frequently, and he hadn't visited her in two weeks. Plus, she'd had to initiate this visit. *Maybe I've pushed too hard—but I'm not getting any younger. I know we have nothing in common, and he lives on a godforsaken island, but he's handsome AND a trust fund baby to boot, so he's definitely the one for me.*

She had two days to plan. She could pull together some fabulous outfits … She bit her lip. *Hmmm, that could be a waste on Whisper Island.* Anyway, she could find something sexy to wear. She would be flexible and let him set the agenda, and she would be as *sporty* as she could bear. She shuddered. Anyway, she'd get things back on track.

She observed a young brunette woman approach her cosmetics counter. With practice honed over time, Chrystal automatically began categorizing the woman by style and ability to pay. Her job as a cosmetic rep paid a salary plus commission on products sold. Chrystal was skilled at her job and highly motivated. Her modeling gigs were drying up, and this Neiman

Marcus job and ad hoc makeup consultations kept her lifestyle afloat. She made eye contact with the brunette and flashed her full wattage smile. Experience had taught her that the more attractive her clients judged her to be, the more money they spent at her counter.

On Saturday, Chrystal disembarked on Whisper Island and spotted Greg's Land Rover in the parking lot. He materialized beside her as she accepted her suitcase from the attendant. "Hey, babe," she said, leaning over to give him a kiss that she deliberately let linger.

"How was your flight? I know the weather is pretty cloudy today."

"All good, thank you for handling the plane ticket."

"Not a problem," he said, reaching over and taking the handle of her suitcase from her grasp. So, there's a chance of rain here—you might be spared a kayak adventure."

"Damn, and I was so looking forward to it," she said dryly, and Greg responded with that low chuckle that she always found sexy.

He opened her car door and went around to the back to load her suitcase. Inside the car, she smoothed her hair in the reflection of the visor mirror and smiled to herself. *Maybe I can avoid all sporty adventures …*

The drive to his home took no time at all, and within minutes, they had pulled up to his sprawling waterfront house. In the year they had been dating, Greg had invited her here only once before. He regularly opted to meet at her place in Seattle, suggesting there was more to do there that she would enjoy.

It was true—she preferred nightlife and elevated dining—but, with her newfound awareness that she needed to up her game, she wondered if there had been more to it than that.

He had retained the basic structure of his family home, gutted the interior, and added two wings on either side of the original structure, blending the old with the new. The exterior featured a combination of cedar-shake and clapboard siding, with various prominent gables that added to the home's personality. The sloping green lawn led directly to the waterfront, and off to the side was a dock where he kept a boat and other water toys.

He left his car parked in the driveway and, retrieving her suitcase, followed her to the front door, opening it for her to enter first. The home featured an open floor plan, and the first impression was one of tall ceilings at varying heights and angles. The ceilings helped define the open space into separate rooms using a mix of materials: stained wood with planks, white painted wood with planks, and some simply plaster with planks. The entryway had a long, narrow table with a few large vases and oversized books. Above it was a wide painting of an empty kayak on a lake. The walls of the house were light-colored but heavily textured, and the furnishings were a mix of cognac-colored leather couches and cream-colored armchairs, all anchored by large neutral rugs positioned over the wide-plank white oak floors. The walls were filled with large, bold artworks. Chrystal could see the kitchen, which featured a rustic, whitewashed brick wall, oversized pendant lighting over an organic wood table, and high-end stainless-steel appliances.

It was a lot for one man, and it made her uncomfortably aware that his long-term plans likely involved children and maybe even pets! *Any wealthy man is going to want the same*, she reminded herself. *Yeah, but they don't all live in the wilderness …* Leaving her suitcase by the door, Greg passed her, heading to the kitchen.

"Would you like anything to drink?" he offered.

"Sure, babe; I'll have a sparkling water with lime?"

"Coming up. Oh, if you'd like to freshen up, I can carry your suitcase up now and then make you a drink?"

"Sure, that would be nice," she said, smiling at him. A thought had just occurred to her, and this would allow her to put it into motion. She sensed an off vibe between them and needed to fix it.

Gentleman that he was, he set the glass down on the counter and, grabbing her suitcase, he started up the stairs. Chrystal followed behind him, carrying her purse. At the door of his room, he set her bag inside and told her to take her time.

She listened to make sure he was heading back down the stairs before she opened his closet door. Dim lighting came on, highlighting rows of suits, dress shirts, and more casual clothes, as well as rows of shined shoes. Chrystal groaned in jealousy. She snatched up a dress shirt and left the closet, shutting the door behind her. In his large and elegant primary bath, she hurriedly stripped off all her clothes, putting on his dress shirt over her naked body. Taking a quick peek at herself in the mirror, she saw that the length skimmed her thighs. She left the first two buttons open at the top and ran a brush through her blonde hair.

She left his bedroom and started down the hall toward the stairs. In her experience, men went crazy seeing a sexy woman in a man's dress shirt. When she was about a third of the way down the steps, Greg turned and saw her. *Was that a slight hesitation?* She watched him set her full glass of sparkling water back down on the counter and begin walking toward her. *I must have imagined it ...*

She had planned on playing the aggressor again, given that she had taken on the seducer role by wearing his shirt, but Greg didn't give her the chance to make the first move. He followed her up to his room and all but threw her down on the bed, ripping at the buttons while pushing the material up her naked thighs. In response, she pulled him down and managed to roll on top of him, pinning him down with her thighs. She rose above him, unzipping his pants, freeing his very hard penis and taking him deep into her mouth. She used her lips, her tongue, and her teeth to drive him to a frenzy, but he managed to pull himself free and, flipping her on her back, he pushed himself into her. A moment later, they each found their release. Wrapped in his arms, she allowed herself a small, satisfied smile. *That should give him something to think about ...*

By Sunday afternoon, Chrystal realized she was enjoying the weekend more than she'd expected. Saturday night, Greg had made reservations for dinner at the Island Resort Hotel, and Sunday morning, he made her a cheese omelet, which was clearly an upgrade from the toast and yogurt she had offered him in Seattle.

Because the weather was still iffy, they hung out on his back terrace with an infinity pool and hot tub, a fire pit, and a large-screen TV. With her permission, he turned on the Seattle Mariners game and brought out a charcuterie tray and white wine for them to share. All in all, it had been a good day, but she still couldn't shake the feeling that something was off.

When Greg surprised her by suggesting that they clean up and head out to a local pub for some live music, she was up for it. Pubs weren't her style, but live music might be fun even if it was from a "nowhere pub."

Chrystal could hear the music as soon as Greg parked, and she opened the car door. It was a slow country croon, and she almost laughed out loud—she should have expected that. They took a seat at a corner table, and Greg ordered drinks while she perused the menu to see what she might want to eat. She had just shut the menu and glanced up at him when she saw his attention snap to the entryway.

She turned her gaze to the door just as three people entered the pub. She didn't recognize the man, or the woman he walked in with, but she did recognize the slender, auburn-haired woman who followed them in. *Sure, that's Rheagan, her fiancé was Greg's best friend … and he was killed in an accident several months ago.* The threesome took seats on the other side of the bar. Greg turned his attention back to Chrystal, and they placed their order—a grilled chicken sandwich and sparkling water for her, and a burger and another beer for him.

"Chrystal, I'm going over to say hello to some friends. You're welcome to join me, and I'll introduce you."

She was about to remind him that she had met Rheagan, and in fact, Rheagan and Mike had joined them for lunch once, but instead, she decided to stay at the table. She wanted to observe him with the group and see if she could better understand that look he'd had when the other woman walked in. "I'll stay here, thanks," she said, and he nodded before making his way over to the group.

It was difficult to draw any conclusions from the interaction. As Greg approached, smiles spread across their faces, followed by what seemed like small talk. At one point, Greg did grasp Rheagan's shoulder, and the two of them shared a smile that seemed to convey something more significant. Chrystal had to admit that it could have been the innocent gesture of one friend to another, both of whom had shared a related loss. She studied the other woman; she was definitely attractive, with long, full auburn hair and unique eyes. *She could cause issues,* Chrystal decided.

Greg returned to their table, and their food arrived, creating a distraction. Chrystal kept up a steady stream of conversation, but even so, she noticed that Greg's attention returned more than once to the table across the room. Another man had joined the threesome and may or may not have been with Rheagan. Still, she didn't like that Greg's attention seemed focused on them. *Or more likely, on Rheagan.* Chrystal tossed her hair back and was considering her options when she saw Rheagan head to the ladies' room. Instinct kicked in, and Chrystal excused herself and headed that way. When Rheagan exited the stall and turned to wash her hands, she saw Chrystal, and recognition dawned in her eyes.

"Hello Rheagan, I saw you and wanted to tell you how sorry I am for your loss."

"Thank you, Chrystal. That's very kind of you."

Chrystal leaned closer and tried her best to conjure up an expression of abashed delight. "Rheagan, please forgive my timing. I just had to tell someone, and when I saw your face, I realized you're at least someone I know. I just took a pregnancy test and … Greg and I are pregnant! I don't want to tell him right now because it's too soon, but I couldn't keep it to myself. I'm sure you can keep my secret."

Rheagan's expression was hard to decipher—surprise for sure, bewilderment maybe? "Umm, sure, congratulations,

Chrystal. You must be very excited." Rheagan turned to the sink and began washing her hands.

Chrystal paused, thrown off by Rheagan's quiet politeness. "Well, see you around," she mumbled, opening the door and exiting. *Yeah, that was awkward. I hadn't planned on telling her that. But a girl with no money has to think on her feet.*

Back at the table, she remained aware of Greg's eyes drifting across the room, but when they prepared to leave, he only lifted his hand in a brief goodbye gesture to the table. Chrystal followed him out and leaned on his arm on their way out to his Land Rover.

When they got back to Greg's house, he offered her a glass of wine, and maybe it was in his expression, but Chrystal knew right then that he was planning to break things off between them. *Oh crap! I thought I had more time!* Her instincts kicked into overdrive. *It's showtime, girl . . .* As he handed her the wine, she grabbed his other hand. Looking into his eyes, her own filled with equal parts of sorrow, regret, and inevitability, she said breathily, "Cash is honoring me at his upcoming fashion show." She bit her lip, and her gaze dropped. She took a deep breath and brought her eyes up again to meet his gaze. "He told me that he can't use me anymore—he needs a younger, unknown face for his runways. I really need you to be there to support me." Her eyes began to water. She saw the capitulation in his eyes before he'd even said a word.

They drank their wine, and he asked her a few questions about her years spent working with Cash. Chrystal answered around the very real lump in her throat. She hated that the card she had been forced to play was real to her, but it was all she could think of at that moment. She was truly devastated that Cash was moving her off his squad. It was the end of her modeling career, and she had planned to spend her final night in the spotlight unaccompanied. Sharing her failures was not generally in her best interests, but tonight it had bought her the extra time she needed.

Chapter Eighteen

Rheagan squeezed her eyes shut and took a deep breath, pushing open the door to SeaTac's Tyee High School's Office of the Registrar. A dark-haired girl who looked young enough to be attending the school herself was seated behind a counter. When Rheagan entered, she looked up from some paperwork and smiled at her. A nameplate identified the girl as Kiera. Rheagan smiled back at her and said, "Hello, Kiera. My name is Rheagan Rossi, and I believe my recently deceased fiancé, Michael Carlucci, attended this high school. May I verify this with you and see if anyone on staff might have known him? I hope to have a conversation with them."

Looking troubled, Kiera rose from her chair. "Oh my gosh, I'm sorry. I'll need to check with Ms. Drake, the registrar. Please give me a minute." She turned and disappeared down a short hallway. In a few short minutes, she reappeared, accompanied by an older woman dressed in a conservative navy-blue suit, who looked sympathetically at Rheagan over the top of the reading glasses perched on her nose.

"What exactly are you looking for, Ms. …?"

"Rossi, my name is Rheagan Rossi. I recently lost my fiancé, Mike Carlucci, and I'm in the area today handling other business related to his estate. I wanted to verify that he attended school here and obtain his childhood home address. Ultimately, I hope to speak with someone who knew him when he was younger. I guess I'm just looking for closure."

Ms. Drake nodded regretfully. "I am sorry for your loss. Unfortunately, the privacy rules governing educational institutions are stringent. Do you have any identification and legal paperwork with you?"

Rheagan nodded. "I have my ID, his will, and letters testamentary."

Ms. Drake shook her head apologetically. "I'm sorry, Ms. Rossi, I can't share any information with you without a formal request. If you have an attorney, you could work with him to submit one."

Rheagan nodded. "Since I'm here, is there any chance you could let me look at some yearbooks from 2009 through 2012?" Rheagan wondered if the older woman could read the desperation on her face.

Ms. Drake considered for a moment and then nodded. "Yes, I think we can do that. Kiera, could you please retrieve the yearbooks and set them up for Ms. Rossi in the conference room? Ms. Rossi, would you like any coffee while you look through the books?"

"That would be wonderful, Ms. Drake. Thank you so much."

"I hope you get that closure you're looking for," the older woman said, patting her arm gently as she turned to walk back to her office.

Kiera smiled awkwardly at Rheagan and said, "Follow me, miss. I will take you to the conference room and bring your coffee before I pull the books."

"Thanks," Rheagan said, following Kiera into the small conference room. *Thank God Greg gave me the tip to ask for the yearbooks. I would have been shut down, but instead, I still have a chance to find out what I need.*

Rheagan glanced mindlessly at her phone notifications while she waited for Kiera. Chrystal's bombshell from the night before kept echoing in her ears. *Greg's about to be a father … Why do I feel so anxious about that? I'm just protective of him, that's all.* Rheagan shook her head to clear it when Kiera returned with a cup of coffee, sugar packets, and some non-dairy creamer, setting them on the table and then darting back out the door. In a few minutes, she returned with the four Tyee High School yearbooks. Rheagan thanked her and opened the first annual. *I need to focus on why I'm here.*

She found Mike's freshman picture easily. It hurt to look at his earnest young face. He wasn't smiling, which didn't surprise her. Mike was intense, but had he always been? *Maybe he chose this photo because his eyes were closed in the smiling one?* She carefully looked through all the photos of sports teams and school clubs but didn't see his picture or his name. Setting the first yearbook aside, she picked up the second.

It wasn't until the last book, his senior year, that she saw him in a baseball team photo wearing a Tyee High School Titan's jersey, and for the first time in his school pictures, he was smiling. The photo also included the team's Coach, J. Scott. Rheagan used her phone to search Tyee High's website and saw that Coach J. Scott was still on staff and, in addition to coaching baseball, taught biology. Tossing her empty coffee cup in the trash, she scooped up the four annuals and made her way to Kiera's desk.

"Hi Kiera, thank you so much for your time and the coffee. Here are the yearbooks—they were very helpful. I was able to find his picture in all of them," she said softly.

"Oh, miss, I am sorry," Kiera said sincerely. She looked over her shoulder briefly and then, meeting Rheagan's eyes, she passed a small piece of paper in her direction. Startled, Rheagan picked it up as Kiera said, "Bye now," and deliberately turned her attention back to her computer.

Rheagan waited until she was down another hallway before she looked at the paper that Kiera had passed her. It was a handwritten note with an address: 1016 Circle Heights Drive, Unit B, SeaTac, WA. *This must have been Mike's home address during his high school years.* With a sigh of gratitude, Rheagan tucked the note into her purse.

It was a school day, and classes were in session. Rheagan turned down a long hallway that still smelled of floor cleaner and saw a hall monitor leaning against a doorframe. She approached and asked where she could find Mr. Scott's biology class. The young girl pointed to a closed door at the end of the hall, and thanking her, Rheagan headed toward it. Hopefully, she would be able to have a quick word with the teacher when class let out. She felt a slight pang of guilt—she was pretty sure that Ms. Drake would disapprove of her actions.

After a few minutes, the bell rang. The door to the biology class opened, and students began spilling into the hall. Rheagan stayed out of the way until she figured the room must be empty. When she peered in, she spotted an older version of Coach J. Scott. His hair was grayer and considerably thinner now. He stood at the front podium, writing something, and he looked up when he heard Rheagan approach.

"Can I help you?" he asked.

"I hope so … My name is Rheagan Rossi. I recently lost my fiancé, Mike Carlucci, in a vehicle accident. I believe you coached him in baseball in 2012. I was hoping you could share some memories with me. I'm just trying to get some closure," she murmured, holding his gaze.

As she spoke, she saw his expression shift. It had been years since Mike had been on his baseball team, so he was probably trying to place him. However, she thought she saw recognition, followed by a sense of sadness.

"I'm sorry to hear that," he said slowly, putting the pen down and turning to face her fully. "Mike was a quiet kid and a natural baseball talent. I wish I could have kept him on the team."

"So, he just played for you his senior year."

Coach Scott shook his head. "It was unfortunate. He tried out and made the team each year, but something always came up, and he pulled out every time. His senior year, too. He just stayed with the team longer that time."

"What kept coming up?" Rheagan asked, her stomach tightening.

"Family issues, but he was always reluctant to talk about them. I think his home life was tough. I tried to speak to him about it, but he was evasive, and I didn't want him to stop coming around. Sometimes with kids, it works better to offer them a welcome place to hang out than to try to force them to talk …" His voice trailed off, and the bell rang, signaling that the next class was starting soon. "I don't have anything else to add. Again, I'm very sorry for your loss. He was too young."

Students began filing into the classroom, and Rheagan knew her time was up. She thanked the coach and walked out the door and down the echoing hall to the school exit. She had accomplished everything she could here. She might have been able to find another teacher, but it would have taken sifting through the website or trying to catch the coach again and asking him who else she could talk to. If Mike hadn't opened up to his coach, she couldn't imagine he would have talked to anyone else. Coach Scott had seemed like a good man.

Chapter Nineteen

Leaving the high school building, Rheagan noticed the sun was surprisingly bright for spring in the greater Seattle area. She opened the door of her rental and sat inside, staring out the window, grateful for a moment to regroup. *It's confusing to grieve Mike and feel distant at the same time.* The pictures and the discussion with Coach Scott had only added to her fears that she may not have really known Mike at all.

She pulled out the paper Kiera had given her earlier and typed the address into the rental car's navigation system. Perhaps she would gain even more insight into the puzzle. As she drove away from the high school, she paid attention to the neighborhoods, and she could see what Greg had warned her about. SeaTac had some rough areas, and it looked like Mike had grown up in one of them.

The navigation system alerted her that she had arrived at her destination. Pulling the car to the side of the road, she studied the building at 1016 Circle Heights Drive, Unit B. It was a worn, white clapboard duplex. *This is another long shot,* she acknowledged as she opened her car door and began walking toward Unit A. She noticed the unmistakable faded chalk outlines of a hopscotch game on the sidewalk to her left. It made her feel better to see that children were playing games and having fun in this tired-looking neighborhood. Maybe Mike had enjoyed good times here, too.

Rheagan rang the doorbell to Unit A, and there was silence. She rang it again, praying to hear answering footsteps. She heard a creak from the side of the house as an elderly woman wearing a bright, flowered house dress came through a gate, carrying a blue plastic watering can.

"Can I help you?" she asked, her faded blue eyes looking inquisitively at Rheagan.

"Yes," Rheagan said in a rush, her relief at seeing the older woman almost making her lightheaded. "My name is Rheagan Rossi, and I want to talk to you about a young man who used to live next door. His name was Michael Carlucci, and the last year might have been 2012 or so. I was his fiancée—he was killed recently in a vehicle accident … and I …" The older woman's shocked look made Rheagan's eyes fill with tears.

The woman came close, patting her gently on the arm. Setting the watering can down, she reached around Rheagan, opening the front door. "Please come in—don't just stand there," she invited. "My name is Emily, Emily Lawrence and, yes, I knew Mike as much as he would let anyone, I guess."

As Rheagan followed Emily into her home, she was greeted by the welcoming smell of something baking. She was led through a tidy living room and into a homey kitchen, which seemed to be where Emily spent most of her time. A large jar filled with fresh flowers sat on the table, along with a small TV tuned to a game show.

Emily bustled in and turned off the TV. "Well, well, where are my manners? Sit, sit—and let me get you a cup of coffee and a piece of my freshly baked banana bread."

“Thank you, Emily. I would love that, and I appreciate your time.” The older woman’s warm nature was a comfort, and the break would give her more time to regain her composure.

Emily nodded her head and indicated for Rheagan to take a seat at the large, scarred wooden table. She stopped at the counter to fill two large mugs with coffee. She handed one to Rheagan along with a sugar bowl and a pitcher of milk. Emily went back to the counter and returned shortly with two plates of warm banana bread. When she sat down across from Rheagan, she reached over and patted her arm again. “This news pains me, my dear. What are you hoping that I can tell you?”

“Mike and I were together for four years. When he passed away, and I cleaned out his things, I didn’t find any personal mementos.” She paused and looked into Emily’s eyes.

“That is odd, you poor thing,” Emily agreed, reaching over to squeeze Rheagan’s hand.

Rheagan took a sip of the coffee, trying to ground herself. The warmth felt good, and after a moment, she said, “I found that he had been keeping some items in a safe-deposit box a good distance from our home, so obviously meant to remain secret. These items were in there.” Rheagan pulled the envelope from her purse. She handed the two pictures to Emily. “Was this his mother?”

Emily reached for her reading glasses and peered intently at the photos of the young dark-haired girl. “When I knew Anna, she had short blonde hair, let me think …it was always dark at the roots, so maybe she was coloring it? I never did think of her as pretty, not like this young girl. That Anna, she always had a sullen look on her face and a cigarette in her hand. I do hate to gossip, but she was the type of woman who felt like life owed her something.” Emily had lowered her voice.

"Maybe because of the cancer?" Rheagan offered.

"Cancer, what cancer? Why, as far as I ever knew, her health was tip-top—she was just an alcoholic, was what she was. And to be honest, Mike took care of her, rather than the other way around, as it should have been. My husband, Frank, and I hated to see what Mike had to endure with that woman." Emily shook her short gray curls. "I didn't like her one bit. But I tried not to let her know because she was vindictive enough to have kept Mike from coming over to visit us, and God bless that poor boy—he needed someone on his side. During his senior year of high school, things were getting just terrible. She wasn't able to work, and that poor Mike was working odd jobs to buy groceries. I tell you, Frank and I were so relieved when his uncle came and took him to live with him."

"So, Mike went to live with an uncle? Was that after Anna died?" Rheagan's head was swirling as she tried to reconcile what Emily was saying with what Mike had told her over the years.

"My dear, Anna didn't die—at least not that I know of. She was here at least two weeks after Mike left. Then that unit went up for rent, and one day, she just drove away and never came back. She left almost everything in the house, she did. Some men with a truck had to come and clear it all out."

Emily reached over and squeezed Rheagan's hand again, and her faded blue eyes were filled with concern. "Honey, you look pale. I reckon this isn't what you were hoping to hear?"

"Emily, nothing I have learned since Mike died has been what I expected," Rheagan said with a broken sigh. "I don't know why he told me his mother died …"

"Maybe telling you that she died was easier than telling you the truth … So, he never did mention his uncle?"

"No, he didn't. Did he ever talk about his father?"

Emily shook her head. "No, never. I always thought his father must never have been around to begin with."

Rheagan nodded sadly. "What was he like, as a boy, when you knew him?"

"They moved next door when he was eleven, I think. He was a lovely boy. So handsome and exceptionally driven, too. I suppose he realized even then that he wanted a different life for himself. But Anna, why she was paranoid and didn't like him to have friends, so he spent a lot of time with us. Frank and I loved that boy, we did. I knew he did the cooking over there, so I taught him how to make the old Norwegian recipes that I grew up with. He surprised me, really took to it."

Rheagan interrupted with a small sob. As tears welled in her eyes, she said, "Thank you, Emily, for being there for him, you and Frank. You should know that he became a very talented chef, maybe because of you."

"Oh goodness gracious! We always wondered about him—we never did hear from him after he left. We both wanted so much for him to do well."

Rheagan smiled proudly. "You'll be pleased to know he went to UW on a full scholarship. In his first year, he met another student, Greg, and they became very close friends, almost like brothers. Mike spent summers and holidays with Greg and his family. He made a career shift and went to culinary school, and that's where we met."

"Oh, it does my heart good to know that he was happy. But it hurts to know that he is gone now." Emily's eyes were full of tears, too.

Rheagan took a deep breath. "Emily, I also found an old ticket stub from a Minnesota Twins game, along with the pictures in that safe-deposit box. Do you recall any conversations about the Twins?

"Oh my, Mike loved baseball. Why, it was his favorite sport. But Anna was always too needy to let him have the time he needed to play. But no, my dear, I don't recall anything about the Twins. He was a Seattle Mariners fan as far as I knew. Rheagan, my dear, please eat some of that banana bread—that and the coffee will warm up your insides."

Rheagan nodded and took a bite, surprising herself by enjoying the food and Emily's warm company.

Greg had insisted on buying Rheagan a seaplane ticket, and she had gratefully accepted. Waiting for the ferry would have meant spending the night in Seattle, and she just wanted to be back in her familiar home at the end of the day. She tried to focus on the adventure of being in a seaplane, but her mind was full of what she had learned about Mike and the discrepancies she had discovered. Hearing of Mike's hardships while growing up made her sad. Did it also help to explain some of his personality traits? *If Mike wasn't nurtured, maybe that was why he seemed disinterested in emotional connections with others … If he had a past that he didn't want to talk about, did he also not want to hear about others' histories?* Emily had described him as driven, and she herself had known him to be intense and sometimes rather selfish with his thirst to experience life. Most disturbing, though, was that it still didn't explain the existence of the safe-deposit box and the pictures that might be of his mother.

Before boarding the plane, Rheagan had texted Greg to let him know she was okay and when she expected to be home.

They had tentative plans for him to drop by her apartment tonight. She gave a heartfelt sigh. Greg's presence in her life meant a great deal to her. Her mind flashed to that bizarre interaction with Chrystal at the bar on Sunday night. *Why am I this upset over her news?* Rheagan was puzzled that Chrystal would share the news of her pregnancy with her before Greg. The two of them barely knew each other and weren't friends. Rheagan hadn't liked seeing her on Whisper Island or with Greg, and she definitely didn't like being asked to keep a secret from Greg. It felt wrong to know something so personal before he did. *I don't want my relationship with Greg to change now that she's pregnant … And how am I going to keep this secret from him?*

Chapter Twenty

Greg looked at his watch—he still had thirty minutes before heading over to Rheagan's place. *I wonder what she discovered today.* Ever since their shared dinner at her apartment, everything he thought he'd known about Mike kept circling through his head. Mike had been his closest friend, truly a brother in any way that counted, yet Mike had evidently kept secrets from him. Why? Greg had drafted his will, and they had discussed Mike's desire to provide Rheagan with the extra life insurance money. His motivations had seemed solely to make sure Rheagan would be as taken care of as possible. *So why leave her to discover secrets on Seal Island?* Greg shook his head in frustration. He had no answers to his questions. He just hoped Rheagan had found something helpful. He didn't like to see that worried look in her eyes.

Since Mike's death, he had been analyzing his own situation as well and had come to some conclusions. Perhaps it was seeing how much Mike had loved Rheagan that made him realize he wanted something more in his life. What he hadn't been prepared for was the dawning recognition that he actually had feelings for his best friend's girl. Spending time with her on all their coffee dates, he had learned to appreciate her intelligence, warmth, and depth. But, even if he could get around the emotional complications of his growing interest in Mike's girl, he might have blown the timing. He had noticed her and Sam having coffee at The Coffee Bean the other day, and had they been together at Jack's pub? Perhaps he would drop in on Sam to gauge their situation.

And I have my own relationship to deal with. Even from the beginning, he had known there was no future in his relationship with Chrystal, but it had served a purpose. She was a beautiful woman, and she could be good company when he wanted that. And because they lived in different cities, they'd each had their independence. However, over time, he had begun to see sides of her that he didn't fully like or trust. It figured that last weekend, for probably the first time in their relationship, Chrystal had seemed genuine right when he'd planned to end things with her. But he'd believed her when she said she needed his support. Perhaps she needed the prop of walking away from the show in front of all her friends on the arm of an eligible man. Whatever her motivation, he had felt like he owed her that. *But now I wish it were over already.*

Greg arrived at Rheagan's front door with a colorful bouquet of tulips and a package of catnip for Mr. Pickles. When he presented them with a flourish, Rheagan laughed, and he was relieved to see that she could find a smile. Maybe her day had been productive.

"Greg, thank you, and come in! You don't need to spoil me by bringing me flowers every time you visit, but Mr. Pickles might be more demanding."

He smelled toasting bread, and his stomach growled loudly in response. He and Rheagan shared another laugh as he followed her down the hall.

"It sounds like you're ready for some apps, and I know I'm ready for some wine!"

She led him into the kitchen, and he could see that she had already set up the island with plates and even lit candles. Opening the oven, she removed a tray of crispy, sliced baguettes and added them to a platter that held a bowl of what looked like a whipped ricotta concoction. Already on the island sat an impressive charcuterie board featuring various cheeses, Italian meats, and an assortment of olives and fresh fruit. While Rheagan placed the now-complete platter on the island, Greg poured pinot noir into their wine glasses.

"Rheagan, thanks for the fantastic spread. I'm getting spoiled by you—my standby of scrambled eggs may not cut it anymore."

"I'm always content when I'm cooking, and I appreciate your company and the chance to talk about my day. Now fill your plate. We can talk while we eat."

They each loaded their plates, and Greg popped a salty olive into his mouth, then immediately asked, "So, how did it go? Sorry, I guess I'm impatient."

She gave him a sad smile. "It was tough. Seeing where he went to school and where he used to live was hard. Telling people who had cared about him that he is gone now was even harder." Her voice broke, and her eyes welled with tears.

Greg reached over and caught her hand in his own, squeezing it before releasing it. "I should have gone with you."

Rheagan shook her head. "I think it was better that I was alone. You were right about the strict privacy rules for schools.

The registrar was very kind, but she wouldn't show me anything without further legal paperwork. I was so thankful that you advised me to ask for yearbooks."

"So, you found his pictures in the yearbooks?"

"Yes, all four years, and Greg, never a smile on his face. In his senior yearbook, he had a picture with the baseball team, and that's the only one where he smiled. And I talked to his baseball coach and his former neighbor, and what they said was disturbing."

"How did you manage to find them if you didn't get any information from the registrar?"

Rheagan gave him a sheepish smile. "I found the coach because the yearbook baseball team picture had his name, and I looked him up on the school website and saw that he was still teaching. A hall monitor directed me to his class, and I waited for the period to end and spoke to him."

"No shit!" Greg shook his head. "That was clever of you."

"It gets better. I got Mike's address because the registrar's assistant felt sorry for me and passed me the information with a sleight of hand as I was leaving."

Greg shook his head again. "I'm impressed. What did they tell you?"

Rheagan's smile disappeared. "His coach told me that Mike made the baseball team every year, and every year, he pulled out because of complications at home. In his senior year, he lasted just long enough to be in the team picture that year. He said he tried to talk to Mike, but he wouldn't open up."

Greg felt a physical pain as he listened to Rheagan's words. He didn't like hearing that his friend had endured hardships in a life that was then cut short.

"When I talked to the neighbor, a lovely older woman, she had nothing good to say about Mike's mom. She described her as vindictive, paranoid, and an alcoholic. It sounded like she wasn't consistently able to hold a job, and in Mike's senior year, he was working to feed them both." Rheagan paused to take a sip of wine, and this time it was she who reached over to cover his hand with her own.

Greg was sure his expression looked bleak, and he struggled to find words that fit his spinning thoughts.

"I know this is hard to hear. I've had several hours to process it all, and you're just hearing it now," Rheagan said softly.

Greg nodded, and she continued to speak. "She described Mike as handsome, lovely, and driven—that she expected him to make something of himself."

Rheagan turned and caught his eyes with her own. "Greg, Emily—that's the neighbor lady—said some things that are inconsistent with what Mike told us. She said that after Mike graduated from high school, he moved in with an uncle. Mike told her and her husband that he was leaving but didn't say where. Mike tended to be evasive, and they had learned not to pry. They saw a man arrive, and the two left together. And … Emily told me that Anna did not die of cancer. Instead, she said that the unit went up for rent and Anna just drove away, leaving everything in the house. A couple of men came and cleared it all away."

"I don't fucking understand any of this!" Greg felt his sorrow morph into frustration. "Did you show her the pictures?"

Rheagan nodded. "Emily couldn't say for sure that it was Anna. She said she had never considered Anna as pretty as the girl in the picture. She said that Anna had short blonde hair, but that she did have dark roots."

Greg sighed, his frustrations spilling out. "So, we have an uncle who, according to Emily, should have been involved in Mike's life at the time I was meeting him in our first year of college. However, he never mentioned an uncle to me, and I never saw evidence of him. We have a mother who didn't die of cancer and could even still be alive. And we've learned that Mike's relationship with his mom may have been more contentious than we thought. So, why, then, keep two pictures of her that he makes annual pilgrimages to? Annual pilgrimages on the date of a baseball ticket stub for a team we didn't know he was a fan of."

"And why keep secrets from us, the two people who loved him?" Rheagan began to cry. Greg reached over, pulling her into his arms. Her body was shaking, and he wished he could say something to help, but he couldn't make either of them feel any better. And he was disturbingly aware that it felt right to hold her.

Chapter Twenty-One

Pennsylvania State Senator A. Luca Bianchi, serving the eighth district, ran his fingers impatiently through his impeccably groomed hair. His dark, wavy strands were beginning to show hints of silver on the sides, which he was okay with. The look gave him a more seasoned and mature persona, which could be a benefit.

"Stefano." He caught the attention of the butler passing in the hallway. "I'm expecting a visitor this evening. I'll see him in here, and Susan shouldn't know he is here." He took a sip of his drink, scotch neat, and welcomed the burn on the back of his throat. He was still dressed in his expensive suit, though he had removed his tie and unbuttoned his collar. Despite the late hour and the company about to join him, he wanted to show who was in control, maybe especially because of the company. His mind wandered to the task at hand. *If only that photo had never been taken, but surely she hasn't kept it all these years?*

He smelled the cheap cologne and cigar smoke before he heard anything. The senator had a visceral reaction—his disdain for Dom had been there since they were kids, playing on the tough streets of South Philly. He gritted his teeth; this unfortunate meeting would be over shortly, and he could open the windows and air the place out. He could make out the footsteps now, the familiar drag in the left leg caused by a "business-related" incident in their youth.

The two men didn't smile or greet each other as Dom entered the room. He hobbled his way across the gleaming wood floor and settled himself heavily into the plush chair across from the senator's desk. "Waddaya need, Luca?"

"I'm exploring a run for governor, which has already been communicated. I need to ensure that certain aspects of my past remain buried, that they can't hurt my image. I'm a married man with a reputation that matters more than ever. I requested you specifically for this job, Dom, because you knew about that unfortunate situation. Angelina informed me that she was pregnant shortly before she left. I need to make sure all ties to that mob hit on her dad, and the existence of a potential child, do not derail my campaign. I know she had at least one photo of the two of us with her pregnancy visible at Franco's Grand Opening—after I'd married Susan. I need you to make certain that photo never surfaces. I can't risk having any ties to that woman." The senator's tone was deliberately curt—this was not a discussion. "Dom, I'm just doing what the boss wanted all along, making sure I have nothing more to do with Angelina. He took care of her dad, now I'm trying to clean up the rest."

He saw no reaction from his late-night guest, but as the man pulled himself up and stood to leave, he turned and spoke in a flat tone, "Luca, ya know the boss, he don' like no surprises. He ain't gonna like that you knocked her up. He got his heart set on you bein' governor. Once youz elected, you can fix things up for us."

The senator ignored him and took another sip of his scotch as Dom left the room. Getting up, he opened the window while reactivating the security system for his sprawling house and grounds. Suddenly, his heart sank. *The ring! I'm such a fool. She would have been wearing it the day of the photo.* He rubbed his head and stared out the window into the darkness. *She can't have saved that photo all these years. Dom will never see it.* He turned from the window and climbed heavily up the stairs to his bedroom suite.

Chapter Twenty-Two

Rheagan came awake to the cold, damp nose of Mr. Pickles pressing against her cheek. "Oh buddy, you don't have any empathy …" Mr. Pickle's unflinching green gaze confirmed his agreement. "You know Saturdays are my late night," she groused, rolling over and trying to ignore him. Light spilled through the white curtains, so Rheagan pulled the fluffy, ivory comforter over her head. Mr. Pickles nudged her again with his nose and began to purr. With a frustrated laugh, Rheagan gave up and reached for her robe on the wicker chair next to her bed.

After feeding her demanding companion, she made coffee for herself and reviewed her schedule for the day. She had an event to prep for that evening, but she still planned to squeeze in a yoga session and maybe some light weight training. Rheagan headed for her bedroom and her workout clothes. As she pulled her sage green yoga top over her head, Mike's engagement ring on her finger caught her eye, and she paused. *Is it time to stop wearing this?* Tears filled her eyes as she realized that taking off the ring felt like another goodbye. "I love you, Mike," she whispered, and slipped off the ring. She walked to her dresser, selected a simple gold chain, and threaded it through the ring, then hung it on her necklace holder. She took a deep breath. *It's time to tackle the day and keep moving forward with Savor.*

She and Charlie from Twisted Sips, the bottle shop, had scheduled their first cross-promotional event for tonight. He had been flexible in planning the event for Sunday night so she could avoid a conflict with her restaurant hours. Charlie had designed three special drinks for the evening: a reimagined mint mojito, a lavender martini, and a basil-infused tequila. Rheagan was bringing complementary appetizers to pair with the drinks: a baked brie with honey and pistachios—served with crostini—as well as clams casino and fried baby artichokes with a squeeze of lemon.

Along with her excitement for the evening was the lingering guilt that flared when she acknowledged that she was moving Savor in directions that Mike would not have wanted. After speaking with Emily, she had gained a better understanding of why Mike had not been a drinker himself and perhaps also why he had not wanted a customer-facing bar in Savor. Still, Rheagan knew that the decision to partner with Charlie felt right. It was another step toward her goal of making Savor feel like her own.

After she finished her coffee, she headed downstairs to the restaurant. She wanted to double-check that she had all the ingredients she needed for tonight, since quite a few were not on the regular restaurant menu. Joe was going to join her later in the day to help with the preparation and serving the appetizers for tonight's event.

Her phone beeped with a text notification, and she snatched it off the counter.

GREG: What are you up to today? Do you want to grab some lunch?

Rheagan felt a zing of electricity at the unexpected invitation. *Oh man … He was already off-limits before Chrystal's confession, and now only more so. Damn Kate for putting thoughts in my head.* She began texting.

RHEAGAN: Would love to but can't today. Charlie and I are doing our XPromo tonight at his shop …

GREG: Oh, right. Mind if I stop by?

She paused for a moment, contemplating, *I'm not sure this is wise,* but her fingers typed anyway.

RHEAGAN: Sure! The promo runs from 6:00 to 7:30, but a few of us plan to stay a bit later. :)

GREG: Sounds great, see you a little after 7.

Rheagan put the phone back down on the counter and tried not to think about electricity, bad timing, and opening herself up to feel again.

Joe laid his knife down and looked at the mound of cleaned and quartered artichokes between them. "This reminds me of culinary school and not in a good way."

Rheagan laughed. "Sorry, they are on the high-maintenance side, but they will be delicious and unexpected. I wish we didn't have to fry them ahead of time, but the tempura batter should help them hold the crunch."

"Agreed. When we did the practice run for family dinner, they held up well on the electric warming plates. Speaking of family dinner, you know the team likes that you've been cooking some of your favorites for our shared meal. I think they're appreciating that the same ingredients we use for our guests can taste very different with an Italian influence."

Rheagan laid her own knife down and turned to Joe. "I've been thinking about making some changes to Savor. To me, the menu that we currently serve doesn't feel cohesive. Though the purpose is to utilize good seasonal ingredients, the inspiration behind the dishes is too broad. For instance, the halibut dish we recently revamped was soy-based but nothing else on our menu has Asian influences. I think you just nailed what I would like to do—I want to put an Italian spin on Savor."

Joe nodded and smiled, warning, "Mannie already worships you—this will only make it worse."

Rheagan laughed, her enthusiasm bubbling up. "Really, Joe. What do you think? Will you work with me on making a new menu?"

Joe paused and tilted his head in that characteristic manner of his as he thought about her words. "Absolutely. I'm excited about it, Chef. Are you thinking rustic Italian, or do you want to stay with the elevated feel of Savor?"

"I think elevated," Rheagan mused, picking up her knife again. "Good. I'm glad we talked about this—it's been on my mind lately."

"Favor to ask, no artichokes on the menu."

"The prep team will back you up on that, I'm sure."

The high Rheagan felt after her conversation with Joe carried her through her yoga session, and she didn't even mind the triceps workout that followed. Her mind was full of creative ideas for the menu. She didn't want to surprise her existing customer base, so maybe she could initially communicate the change on social media. She would also need to update the Savor website.

But first things first—tonight's event. She showered and dressed in skinny jeans and a long-sleeved, V-necked T-shirt. The butter yellow complemented both her eyes and her hair. She applied her makeup, opting for a smoky cat-eye look, and she styled her hair in a smooth high ponytail to keep it out of her way. Her jewelry was simple: layered chains at her throat and silver hoops in her ears. She smiled at her reflection. *It feels good to see myself cheerful and looking my best.*

When she entered Savor, Joe was already there and frying the artichokes. She started on the clams and brie. When they finished the apps, they packed them up along with the warming trays and loaded them into Joe's SUV. The bottle shop was only a short walk away, but with all their gear, they still needed to drive.

As soon as they unpacked, Charlie mixed them drinks of their choice: infused tequila for Joe and a martini for Rheagan. "Yummm, I taste the lavender in the most subtle, amazing way," Rheagan said, impressed.

The crowd was eclectic, a good mix of Savor's customer base along with younger folks who might typically opt for more casual dining. She and Joe were kept busy with the appetizers, and Charlie and his team mixed the cocktails. The music they'd picked set the perfect atmosphere, and people were having a good time.

As it got closer to 7:00 p.m., Rheagan realized that she was watching for Greg to arrive. When she turned around after refilling the artichokes, she noticed him talking to Kate and Jeff. He was wearing a button-down shirt, left untucked over a pair of faded jeans. His hazel eyes caught on hers, and he gave her a slow smile. *Damn, that electricity again … It's apparently a thing …*

He walked over in her direction. "Hey, looks like you still have a good crowd. I'm just hoping you saved me some apps!" His dark blond hair looked ruffled from the wind, and his grin was contagious.

"You're in luck!" Rheagan reached for a plate and loaded it with one of each appetizer, along with a napkin featuring the Savor Logo.

"Nice touch on the napkin," he commented before dipping his artichoke in the sauce and popping it in his mouth. "Oh man, that's delicious," he said after swallowing.

"You should taste them when they're fresh out of the fryer," Joe offered.

Rheagan laughed and looked at Joe, surprised. "Did I hear an opening for artichokes on the menu?"

Joe smiled back at her. "Just bowing to the inevitability. They are damn good!"

Perhaps it was partly due to the cocktails she had been sipping, or maybe it was simply the satisfaction of a good day with Joe, a successful event, and the company of friends, but Rheagan felt happy. *This feels right. Things are good again.*

At 7:30, Charlie put out the *Closed* sign. Most customers had already left, but Charlie offered refills to those who were still enjoying themselves. Rheagan tried a sip of Greg's drink, the basil-infused tequila, and feeling warm and tipsy, was grateful that Mondays were a day off.

After one more drink, Joe told Rheagan he would drive the warming trays back to Savor and do the cleanup. Rheagan protested, but he told her to relax, and she thanked him, deciding to do just that. She and Greg remained behind with Charlie and his girlfriend, debriefing on their shared event. Eventually, they opted to leave, and Charlie gave each of them a to-go cup.

Outside, the spring air was cool and damp with the smell of the marina that Rheagan loved. "I left my Land Rover at Savor," Greg shared. "So, may I walk you home?"

Rheagan nodded, pleased to be in his company and definitely buzzed from the alcohol. At her building, Greg grasped her hand. "Sit with me here on the steps for a minute—it's a pretty night." She allowed him to pull her down with him, and they sipped their drinks companionably.

"It *is* a pretty night—I love Whisper Island," she said. "And that's not just the alcohol talking."

Greg turned to her with a big smile. "So, does this mean that you've decided to stay?"

"Yes, I want to be here—it feels right here in a way that Connecticut didn't. And I'm planning some changes for Savor that feel right to me, too."

Greg nodded and, reaching toward her, brushed back a chunk of hair that had escaped her ponytail. His touch set off delicious shivers of that electric current, but she tried not to let it show.

"I'm really glad you want to stay, Rheagan. I didn't want you to go."

Rheagan had the confusing sense that Greg might be feeling some voltage of his own, and the sadness of bad timing descended on her. *Greg has a girlfriend, and more than that* … She reluctantly tipped her glass against his, hoping to shift the mood. "Thanks for joining me tonight. I should let you go … It's a real Monday for you tomorrow."

"You are right about that," Greg said, rising to his feet and extending a hand down to help pull Rheagan to her feet.

He kept her hand in his as he walked her to the private entrance that led to her apartment. When she opened the door, he brought her close for a hug and wished her goodnight. "Goodnight, Greg, and thanks for coming over tonight. It was fun," she said and closed the door quickly before electricity and alcohol could ignite.

Upstairs in her cozy boho bedroom, she removed her makeup, brushed her teeth, and sat down, holding Mr. Pickles tightly in her arms. She did want to stay on Whisper Island, and that decision had to be her own, not influenced by any feelings that she had for Greg. How strange that she was even thinking like this about him. After Kate had told her about Greg's trust issues with women, she had recalled various conversations with Mike about Greg's dating life. Mike had called Greg's past girlfriends, including Chrystal, the "disposables." *Even though it's a bad idea, it does feel good to feel electricity again …*

Chapter Twenty-Three

Following the success of her event at Charlie's bottle shop, Rheagan turned her focus to moving forward with her plans for Savor. She felt a sense of satisfaction and energy that she knew had been missing from her relationship with her restaurant before. If she were honest with herself, that same optimism was spilling into her personal life as well. She and Greg continued with their weekly walks, and while she did sense that there was a growing bond and yes, even electricity in the air, she did her best to avoid any mixed signals on her part. Most of all, she hated that she was keeping Chrystal's secret.

Now, three weeks later, Rheagan and Joe perched on stools in the *Inspiration Room,* designing the Italian version of Savor. Printouts of the menu, with handwritten notes scribbled on them, were scattered across the wooden table, along with potential recipes and inspo photos.

"Come on, Chef, those meatballs are so good," Joe protested. "You have to put them on the menu."

"Maybe as an appetizer? I love them too, but they just don't feel elevated. They are more like comfort food," Rheagan added.

"Okay, sure, I can see them as an appetizer. I guess that's where the artichokes fit in, too?" Joe flexed his arms, stretching his shoulders after sitting so long.

"Yeah, maybe even just a seasonal starter. I want to continue offering a menu that is based on seasonal, fresh ingredients as much as possible."

Joe tilted his head a moment in thought, then nodded. "Yeah, that sounds right—that's what we've been known for, and that consistency will be good. I think that's what makes the locals choose us over having dinner at the resort."

"Ah, good observation." Rheagan nodded, impressed.

She and Joe had been slowly working through classic Italian recipes to replace existing dishes. Tweaking them, elevating them, and making them, in their opinion, Savor worthy. Today, they were taking on one of her favorites, a chicken Milanese salad. They had already coordinated on a written recipe outline and would later execute it. She was excited to taste the result and see whether they would make further tweaks to the outline.

Joe glanced at the clock on the wall. "Oh man, looks like I'd better head down to the kitchen. I'll catch you later for the salad, Chef?"

"Sure, Joe, thanks for your time."

As he left, she thought, *I'm always impressed with his work. We got lucky when Joe joined the team.* She planned on promoting him to head chef once they had the initial menu in place and had completed the transition of Savor to the new Italian version. He deserved it. She would retain full creative license, but already, Joe was the boss in the kitchen, and his work should be recognized for what it was.

Her eye caught on Mike's CIA manual on the shelf. She realized that whenever she was in the room, she focused on that book as a tangible way to connect with Mike. Whatever she was learning about Mike's secrets, she still believed that he had truly loved her. She wanted to believe that he would have wanted her to be happy now, even if that came from decisions he would not have made for Savor. And even if that happiness meant that she had confusing feelings for his best friend. *I loved you, Mike, despite my concerns—I loved you. And I haven't given up on finding the answers to your secrets. I intend to keep my promise to understand you better.*

Rheagan spent a busy afternoon in her office analyzing the changes needed to her regular ordering process. The shifts were subtle, like introducing more accouterments, such as olives, and upgrading their olive oil to a high-end finishing quality. Although they were still in the testing and development phase, trends were already emerging that she could work with. Savor had been offering some of the new dishes as specials, and the customer feedback had already been enthusiastic. She'd even been toying with the idea of whether they should start making their own fresh pasta.

She was straightening her already neat desktop and filing her papers away when her phone buzzed. She glanced at it, seeing Trey's name. "Hey, Trey, what can I do for you?"

"Chef, may I come up and talk to you for a minute?"

"Sure, Trey, I'm in my office."

"Right. On my way."

Rheagan heard the security system's sound followed by him climbing the stairs. It was rare for him to visit her up here. She smiled to herself as he entered her office door. He was the neatest chef she had ever worked with. He wore his brown hair shorter than most chefs, kept it tidy under his bandana, and rarely had a spot on his white coat.

"Chef," he said, taking the chair across from her desk. He met her eyes with his own blue ones, but he swallowed visibly. "The resort has offered me a job as sous chef." He swallowed visibly again and then said quickly, "I didn't apply—they approached me, but I did meet with them."

Rheagan felt a pang of disappointment, but she had always valued her staff and wanted them to be successful. Growing up in this business, she knew how competitive the restaurant scene could be, and it wasn't unusual for talented staff to move around. "I see," she said, smiling reassuringly at him. "Trey, you are very valued here. I hope you recognize that. Joe was telling me the other day about how strong your technical skills are. I'm sure it's obvious to you and the rest of the team that we'll see some roles shift and promotions here at Savor soon. Can you share with me whether your interest in their offer is related to the title promotion or if you are looking to make a change anyway?"

"Chef, Savor is legit, and I know it's because I've been working here that the resort even reached out to me." His eyes slid away, and he swallowed again, but then he met her gaze. "Chef, I wondered if maybe Manny was going to get the sous chef role here. He's a great guy, and he's thriving under the changes you've been making. I guess I wondered if the resort job would be a safer option for me to grow my career."

Rheagan nodded in understanding. "Manny is very enthusiastic about the changes, and I think he is pushing himself to grow right now. You have chosen to work in a very creative field, and that comes with competition. That competitive drive is what creates space for chefs to shine. You worked under Mike and his vision for Savor, and now you are seeing how my vision is different." Rheagan smiled now. "My advice to you would be to choose the place where you feel challenged and can continue to learn. I can tell you again that you are valued here, and your pay will remain competitive. The decision about the next sous chef will be Joe's, and I hope you will talk to him about it. In any event, congratulations on gaining their interest at the resort, but I do mean this—I hope you will choose to stay with us at Savor."

The family meal debate was ongoing regarding the chicken Milanese salad. "Chef, I think we should go with pure olive oil and a splash of lemon. The ingredients are so good, simplicity is the way to go," Manny stated emphatically.

"Manny, I disagree. Let's go with the vinaigrette, which incorporates the shallots and balsamic vinegar. It's still subtle, but it brings something hard to define and elevates the dish to one that a customer will feel they couldn't replicate at home," Joe countered.

Manny nodded his head, considering Joe's explanation. "I enjoy the coarse grind on the salt too; it provides its own crunch factor."

Joe smiled in Rheagan's direction, and she returned the smile. Manny's enthusiasm and insight had surprised them both. He had a well-developed palette and offered helpful comments.

"I agree with Joe's perspective on the customer," Rheagan said. "We need something a little less basic. Oh, and this panko crust is delicious. Overall, I think this is successful." Several heads nodded in agreement.

"Chef, what do you think about adding a touch of tarragon to the vinaigrette? I realize it's unconventional, but I think a subtle anise flavor might brighten it up. I honestly agree with Manny on how I personally prefer it, but as long as we are looking to elevate the flavor, it would punch it up a notch." Trey spoke from the end of the table.

"Huh, interesting." Rheagan looked at Joe, and they both nodded. "Let's try that before we finalize this."

Upstairs in her apartment after closing Savor, Rheagan removed her shiny black pumps, but this time, she smiled as she put them neatly away in her closet. Maybe she had broken them in, or her feet had grown accustomed to them, but she had managed to survive the evening with relative ease.

She and Mr. Pickles headed to the kitchen, where Rheagan poured herself a glass of wine and made a snack of leftover salad that she'd brought with her from downstairs, along with some cheese from her refrigerator. She had picked up her laptop from her office on the way to her apartment, and opened it on her kitchen island. She must have been subconsciously thinking about the pictures that were presumably of Anna because an idea had occurred to her during the dinner service.

She typed "How can I find the location of a photo taken in the 1990s?" She got a few results that didn't seem helpful, so she typed the question into her AI assistant again. Immediately, she had a few options, some free and a couple paid. *Wow, I think I can do this!* Rheagan clicked on the free website and downloaded the steps. She planned to scan the picture of the young man and the girl with the grand opening banner because it showed what appeared to be a commercial structure and visible lettering. Grabbing her phone, she took a picture of the photo and then sent it to her email address. In a few seconds, the photo appeared, and she uploaded it to the website. Then, she clicked the *Find My Location* button. She took a sip of wine and jolted to attention when her screen updated. Two locations appeared on her screen, along with their probabilities and the criteria used to support the analysis. Rheagan set her wine glass down and pulled the laptop closer to study the results. Each had a street address; the site with the lower probability was in Chicago, Illinois, and the other site, with a significantly higher likelihood, was in Philadelphia, Pennsylvania.

"Damn, Mr. Pickles, I think I'm on to something," she said aloud. She clicked on the paid service site. This site would perform a similar analysis, then take additional steps to reduce or eliminate multiple options. Impulsively, she began entering the required data and uploaded the photo, along with her credit card information. Neither Chicago nor Philadelphia was close to SeaTac, where Mike had grown up. *Am I just going down a rabbit hole?*

Chapter Twenty-Four

Greg awoke to the muted light of morning. Reaching for his phone, he turned off his alarm. Much more pleasant to wake up before it went off and embrace the silence of an early morning on Whisper Island. He was about to start browsing his emails when he noticed he had an unread text message. It was a late-night message from Rheagan asking if she could meet him today at The Coffee Bean at 9:00 a.m. Today wasn't their regularly scheduled morning, and he hoped everything was okay. He quickly texted her back, promising to see her there.

When he pulled into the parking lot, Rheagan was standing there with a coffee cup in each hand. He walked over to meet her, pulled her in for a gentle hug and looked directly into her eyes. They reflected excited impatience, and he exhaled in relief.

"So, you couldn't wait until tomorrow to see me," he teased, accepting the hot black coffee she passed over to him.

"I couldn't! Greg, I may have found something useful, and I wanted to share it with you." She was pulling a folded paper out of her pocket. "I think the picture of the young man and the girl we think is Anna was taken in Philadelphia," she said. "Last night, I had the idea to upload the photo to an AI site, and I got a couple of hits, one for Chicago and one for Philadelphia. I then used a paid site, and this morning, I got this." She reached for the coffee she had just handed him so that he could trade it for the paper.

He unfolded the document and scanned it, seeing the uploaded 'Grand Opening' banner picture of Anna and the young man, along with an address in Philadelphia. The document also listed the criteria used, including the restaurant's opening date. He nodded. "Philadelphia … He never mentioned that city to me. How about you?"

"No, never. Greg, I need to go there."

Greg felt an immediate concern for her and how quickly she was moving on this. He reached out and grasped her arm. "Honey, what do you expect to find in Philadelphia, even if you have an address?" Greg saw Rheagan's eyes snap to his in surprise. *Did I just call her honey? And why does that feel so right?*

Rheagan squared her shoulders. "I want to know more about this girl and why this picture was important to Mike. Greg—it's a family-owned restaurant that has been in operation for many years. I think it's even still the same owner." She pushed her hair behind her ears impatiently. "I want to ask him if he knows this girl. Greg, what if she's Anna? What if she grew up there and maybe even moved back after she left SeaTac?" Her words came out in a rush of what sounded like pure adrenaline, and Greg surmised that this likely wasn't her first coffee.

He shook his head in a cautionary manner. "I guess anything's possible. That's a long way to go, and you might not get any more answers."

Rheagan looked up at him, and her eyes held his. "I have to do this, Greg. I feel as if I need to understand why he kept secrets from me. I feel like it's the last thing I can do for him." Her eyes began to fill with tears, and Greg knew he couldn't stop her, but he wouldn't let her go solo, either.

"Rheagan, I want to go with you on this trip. Mike kept secrets from both of us, and I don't want you to do this alone."

"Greg, are you sure?" Her tone was low and soft. He had the impression that she was both thankful and emotional about his offer to go with her. He felt a rush of protectiveness toward her. He knew that it was more complicated than that as well. And worse, whatever it was, he knew he hadn't felt it for any woman before.

Back at his office, Greg reviewed his calendar—he would need to reschedule some appointments. He should also contact Chrystal and let her know he would be out of town for a couple of days. He debated whether he needed to communicate the trip at all, let alone Rheagan's presence, but until he was able to end things between them officially, it seemed wrong to hide information from her. Deciding to get the conversation over with, he called her cell.

She picked up on the second ring. "Hey, babe, I was just thinking of you ..." she purred breathily.

I am so over her games. I wish I had just ended this on her last visit. "Hey, Chrystal, I'm calling to let you know that I'll be leaving town on Sunday. I need to travel to Philadelphia."

"What's in Philadelphia?" The purr was gone, replaced by an irritated tone.

"Just some steps to follow up with on Mike's death."

"Oh, so is the redhead going with you?"

Greg felt an immediate flash of dislike for Chrystal, and her bitchy comment that he knew was meant to be demeaning. "Mike's fiancée is named Rheagan, and yes, she needs to be there too. It's a short trip—we leave on Sunday and return on Tuesday."

Chrystal had likely recognized his frustration with her because she changed tactics. "Okay, babe," she breathed. "It's just I was counting on seeing you this weekend. Is there any chance you could come up here on Friday? I'm assuming you're flying out of Seattle." Her tone was beseeching now.

"I can't. This trip is unexpected, so I have to rearrange some items on my calendar. I've got to run now. Just wanted to give you a quick heads-up. I'll call you later." Greg disconnected the phone and sighed.

He had insisted on handling the travel arrangements for Rheagan and himself, so he turned back to his computer and pulled up the American Airlines website. He selected the travel days and non-stop flights and groaned when he saw the results. One choice: a red-eye flight out of Seattle on Sunday and either an early-morning flight or a late-afternoon flight on Tuesday. Not ideal, but with Rheagan's Savor responsibilities, he guessed she would choose the early morning return. If they were able to sleep reasonably well on the Sunday red-eye flight, that would give them most of Monday to walk around and have dinner at Michelangelo's Ristorante. He wasn't sure what else they could really discover there anyway. Searches for Anna Carlucci had not been fruitful, so the restaurant was the best chance to find out anything more.

He texted Rheagan the flight options and began searching for hotels. There was a relatively new Four Seasons Hotel in Center City that appeared to offer amazing downtown views. He wanted to make the trip as enjoyable as possible for her. And he admitted to himself that he was looking forward to spending this time with her. He had always admired her confidence and entrepreneurial skills. Mike had been clear that Rheagan was the business brain behind Savor. *Those traits are probably why she also seems to be a talented bloodhound*, he thought with amusement. He was impressed by what she had learned from her trip to SeaTac and how she'd uncovered the photo's location. But as he spent more time with her, it was her genuineness and warmth that really drew him in. *Be honest. There's a strong attraction, too …* Smiling to himself, he booked two rooms for the Four Seasons.

Chapter Twenty-Five

Greg grabbed his phone and pulled up Sam's contact info. He hit the call button and took a sip of his coffee while waiting for his friend to respond.

"Hey Greg, what's up?" Sam said when he picked up.

"Just calling to see if you're interested in taking the kayaks out for an early morning run tomorrow?"

"Ah, my friend, that sounds perfect. The usual, meet at your place at 6:00?"

"That works, and I'll have the coffee and bagels. Looking forward to it."

"See you tomorrow," Sam said, ending the call.

The next morning was perfect for kayaking. The sun was just coming up, and the air was crisp and cool, creating a mist over the water. When Greg saw Sam's truck pull up, he met his friend outside with a bag for each of them containing a YETI filled with hot coffee, a couple of toasted bagels with cream cheese, and plenty of napkins.

Sam grunted as he lifted his kayak off his truck. "Morning, Greg. The water looks perfect."

"Sure does," Greg agreed as they crossed the dewy lawn and walked down to the dock. The two men made quick work of getting their kayaks into the water. They had shared mornings like this since they were young boys, and their combined efforts were practiced and efficient.

On the water, they set off in their usual direction, and Greg felt the natural rhythm of the paddling calm his mind. From his vantage point in the front kayak, Sam held up his hand to direct Greg's attention to a bald eagle soaring above. Looking to the wooded shoreline, he also spotted herons in the shallow water. The two men continued paddling until they reached a protected cove. Greg pulled his kayak even with Sam's, and the two substituted their paddles for coffee mugs.

"How's the farm?" Greg asked.

Usually, Sam addressed that topic in a word or two. This time, he opened up. "More satisfying than I'd imagined it would be. I understand now what my dad always said—it's hard work, and a lot of it is out of your control. But it's also rewarding to see the tangible results of all your hard work. The farm-to-table and organic trends have changed farming a lot, and they are groovy changes to be a part of."

"That's great to hear," Greg said, meaning it. He respected how hard Sam worked, and he was glad to see his friend's passion.

"And how is the law?"

"Honestly, booming. My cases span the entire spectrum, and it keeps me busy because research is essential, which takes time," replied Greg, having taken his cue from Sam in terms of how much to share. "I've been considering that it may be time to hire a paralegal."

"Are you serious, man?"

"Yeah, I've been thinking about it. Why?"

Sam balanced his coffee between his knees and used his hand to pull Greg's kayak closer; his face was serious. "I think Mindy is finding Seattle a little big and impersonal for a single mom. You know that she's a paralegal at a large firm there. Would you be willing to talk to her?"

"Of course! Friendship aside, Mindy is a very bright woman. I'd be happy to talk to her. Are the two of you working on things?"

"We are … Greg, I've always loved that girl, and although I'm not going to say that I'm glad for the divorce, I think she needed to make that move to show herself that being there and in a big firm isn't all that. A life with Amy and me on the farm can be good too."

Greg nodded his head. "I'm happy for you, man, I am. When we get back, shoot me her number, and I'll call her today. I had been wondering if maybe you were interested in Rheagan?"

Sam smiled but shook his head. "Nah, Mindy's my girl, but I have serious respect for Rheagan. When I say that farming is getting more interesting now, it's because of chefs like her. She is clever and creative. I can tell you for a fact that her kicking ass on Whisper Island has elevated the resort's game. It's obvious based on the orders they've been placing with me since Savor opened. And now she's changing up the menu and focus of Savor, and I'm totally a fan. In fact, I thought you might be interested in Rheagan," Sam said, looking pointedly at him. "I've known you a long time, my friend, and I sense a vibe."

"Ah, yes, I am interested in her … but I have to end things with Chrystal."

Sam brought his kayak close again. "Man, maybe I should have told you this before, but I didn't want to cause trouble, and I never thought you had serious intentions for Chrystal anyway." He cleared his throat awkwardly. "I'm not sure it makes sense to say it now, but maybe you should know. Mindy said she saw Chrystal in a bar with another guy a couple of times. She said they looked pretty intense."

Greg nodded. "I'm glad you told me, Sam. Our relationship was supposed to be exclusive, so I am surprised on one level, but there are sides to her that she hides. That information could be helpful when I talk to her. Seriously, thanks, man."

A pod of porpoises swam by, and both men turned to enjoy their frolicking antics. After finishing their breakfast, they resumed their exploration of the familiar waters before turning their kayaks back in the direction of Greg's house.

As he paddled home, Greg felt the satisfaction of a solid workout and quality time with a good friend. *I'm glad Sam and Mindy are working on things—hopefully, my offering her a job will help.* He also acknowledged his relief that he hadn't missed his chance with Rheagan. As for the Chrystal thing, maybe it would make their conversation easier.

Chapter Twenty-Six

Pennsylvania State Senator A. Luca Bianchi finished his speech, and the packed theater erupted into a deafening roar of enthusiastic applause. Nodding graciously at the numerous faces, the handsome, dark-haired man held up his hands in acknowledgment and exited the stage behind a red velvet curtain. The security team was waiting along with his top advisor, Doug Knowles. The group headed out a backstage door and climbed into a waiting limousine.

"Excellent speech, sir," Doug said tentatively. "You've gotten these people stirred to a frenzy tonight. This type of momentum is exactly what we need to build on."

"Yes, Doug, it's what I do best," the senator said smugly. "And you're right, of course—what we need are a lot more of these types of opportunities …" The senator's voice faded off as he lost himself in a vision of his shining future. *A few more speeches like this,* he thought, *and I'll have the governorship.*

The limousine began to move down the brightly lit street, inching its way through the sea of people, their hands outstretched and their faces shining with the dream that Senator A. Luca Bianchi was offering. There was a sudden jolt as the driver was forced to stop abruptly for a group of supporters who were crossing the road, chanting, "Bianchi for Governor" over and over in unison.

"Oh, for God's sake," the senator said, his mouth thinning in contempt. "Why don't these people just get out of the way?" The limousine broke free and began to move forward again; soon, the crowd of chanting, waving people was visible only in the rearview mirror.

Twenty minutes later, the limousine pulled up in front of a stately brick mansion. Senator Bianchi waited as the driver hurried to open the car door for him. "Goodnight, Doug. Let's touch base in the morning," he said over his shoulder while exiting the car. Another car door opened, and the senator's security detail exited the vehicle, walking beside him to his well-lit entrance.

"Thank you, Ed. Take the night off. I am safely home and in for the remainder of the night."

"Sir, I am happy to stay." The security detail opened the front door, stepped inside, and performed a quick sweep of the area.

"No, Ed, I don't need you here."

Ed nodded. "Good evening, sir."

The door closed behind the agent, and the senator bit back his anger. He could smell the damn cigar and cheap cologne from where he stood. He made his way to his study, ignoring the large man sitting in the dark corner. He went directly to the scotch and poured a double, taking a sip before even taking his seat behind the desk.

"We found her, Luca. She's livin' in LA an' usin' her real name," Dom said with no inflection in his voice.

"Jesus Christ!" the senator erupted.

"Got nuttin on a kid. We're gonna go in soon, so we'll get more. Oh, an' Luca, the boss, he's gonna want a favor from ya soon." The threat was delivered in that same flat tone.

Dom got up slowly from his chair and headed for the back exit.

The senator waited until he heard the other man's uneven gait leave the house, then reactivated the security system. He moved immediately to pour himself another double before sitting down again. He didn't like that Angelina was using her real name again. Perhaps she felt she had nothing left to lose. That might not bode well for his campaign. On the other hand, she had been easy to find because of that fact.

In his scotch-permeated state, he recalled the beautiful young girl he had known. *Just like Dom, she didn't know her place,* he mused sullenly. His mind moved to the warning Dom had delivered on his way out, and his hand shook a little as he raised the glass to his lips for another sip. It wasn't easy to deliver on favors … *and my track record isn't good,* he acknowledged. He quickly took another swallow of his scotch.

Chapter Twenty-Seven

Greg had brought a red-eye care package for Rheagan and himself to help them get some rest on the flight. Her package included a cashmere throw, a sleep mask, and earplugs. Seated in her first-class seat beside him, he watched as Rheagan smoothed her fingers over the soft pink blanket and luxuriated in its softness, even bringing it up to her face to feel the texture against her cheek. *It's fun to offer her gifts because she always expresses such appreciation and joy.* He smiled to himself, then his heart stilled for a moment when he realized she was no longer wearing Mike's engagement ring. *Ah, Rheagan, that must not be easy. I know how much you loved him.* Greg admired her strength and determination to make the most of the life she had.

A flight attendant came by to offer them a choice of a cheese plate or a hummus plate, along with their drink of choice. They each ordered the cheese and a red wine. Rheagan took a sip of her Cabernet and turned to him, "Thank you again for handling all the travel and accommodations, not to mention this lovely surprise," she said, indicating the blanket.

"It was my pleasure. I enjoy doing things for you, Rheagan. You are such an amazing hostess when I come over. This is my way of thanking you." She seemed touched by that and reached out to squeeze his forearm.

"I especially thank you for getting me the pink blanket. People often assume I avoid pink because of the red in my hair, but I love anything pink." She smiled happily.

"Your hair is such a mix of colors, dark brown, gold, and those shots of red fire," Greg said, reaching over to push a strand back from her face. He noticed again how silky her hair always felt.

"Yes, a mix of my Italian father and my Irish mother," she said, and her smile reflected the warmth and affection she had for her parents.

"I'm Scandinavian on both sides."

"That explains why you have so much blond in your hair." Rheagan nodded. She reached out again to touch his hand this time. "I'm sorry about the loss of your parents—it must be tough to have them both gone from your life."

"Thank you, I still miss them. They were wonderful and always so devoted to each other. I don't think my dad really ever got over losing my mom to her stroke."

The reflective mood was broken by the flight attendant stopping by to clear their trays and offer them another beverage. They both declined, and Rheagan settled back into her chair with the pink blanket pulled up snugly around her shoulders. After just a few minutes, he was pretty sure she'd drifted off to sleep. He smiled at how the throw managed to cover her petite frame while his own long body was uncovered from the knees down.

The town car delivered them to the iconic Comcast Towers in Center City, Philadelphia. Entering the one that housed the

Four Seasons Hotel, the express elevator whisked them to the hotel desk on the sixtieth floor. Greg handled the check-in; he had booked an extra day so rooms would be available upon their arrival. When he turned back to find Rheagan, he saw her facing out the window, enjoying the sweeping skyline.

"It's like we're in the clouds," she said in awe. "I can't wait to see this view in the dark."

Greg smiled too. "It is incredible—let's go see the view from our rooms." Grabbing her free hand, he led her to the elevator and used his key card to send the elevator to the fifty-eighth floor. Their rooms were next to each other, both modern yet plush, in grays and blues, with floor-to-ceiling vistas.

"Wow!" Rheagan exclaimed, walking toward the window. "We're so high, it almost doesn't look real!"

Her face was animated, and Greg felt a warmth inside at her ability to enjoy the moment. "How do you want to spend the morning, Rheagan? Do you need a couple more hours of sleep, or do you want to get ready and find some breakfast?"

Rheagan turned to look up at him as she touched his shoulder. "You, my friend, look exhausted. Why don't we make the most of these comfy rooms and get some rest? Do you want to meet for lunch at noon?"

"That works, just knock on my door when you're ready, and I will see what I can find for a good lunch spot," Greg said, walking to her door and letting himself out.

It was only spring, but the East Coast, Philadelphia included, seemed to have a gentler take on that season than the dreary Northwest. The concierge had made lunch reservations for them at Parc, a French bistro in Rittenhouse Square. They had each worn light jackets, so they took the opportunity to sit outside on wicker chairs under the sidewalk awning and watch locals enjoying the renowned Philadelphia Square. Greg was glad to see that Rheagan looked well-rested. *She also looks so pretty with her long hair loose and blowing in the gentle breeze.* He wondered if these complex feelings for Rheagan had always been in the background, even before Mike's death. He thought maybe they had.

"Greg, this variety breadbasket is amazing. Have you tried the one with the walnuts, and I think these are cranberries? Mmm … delicious." She broke off an end and handed it to him. "I also love how they serve flaky salt on the butter."

Greg accepted the bread from her and took a bite. "That is good! And, this Sancerre is delicious too, nice minerality. Maybe we should take red-eye flights across the country for lunch more often."

Rheagan laughed. "Maybe we can skip the red-eye part."

After a long, drawn-out meal, they walked around for a bit, enjoying the historic neighborhood, and browsed through a few shops on Walnut Street. Finally, they wound their way back to the hotel. Greg walked Rheagan to her door and, looking down at her, he said in a low voice, "I hope we find the answers we are looking for."

She reached out to touch his arm and, looking into his eyes, she said, "At least I'll know we tried."

Chapter Twenty-Eight

Chrystal rolled over, pulling the sheet up to cover her naked breasts. Cash gave a low, amused laugh. "What's with the modesty? I've seen them before, and we both know I'll see them again." Chrystal sighed in annoyance but not necessarily in disagreement. She and Cash had history and an understanding.

Cash reached over and gave her a light, affectionate kiss on her lips before pushing himself into a sitting position. "We're good together, Chrystal. We may not check all the boxes on either of our "lists," but we understand each other. We know what makes each other tick, and we're probably each other's oldest and most loyal friend."

Chrystal looked at him while he spoke, but she didn't reply.

"What? You don't think I'm loyal just because I'm pulling you from the show line-up?" Cash asked, looking down at her.

Chrystal still didn't reply. She was unable to speak around the lump in her throat.

"Babe, that's business, not personal."

"So is my modeling career just over?" she asked in a wobbly voice, trusting him to tell her the truth.

"That is your choice, honey," he said, gently pushing a strand of blonde hair out of her eyes. "You could do print."

"Sure, posing with children in local retail store circulars or catalog work." Her tone had turned petulant.

"Maybe, but you'd be making a living doing what you want to do. You're a beautiful woman in a career that ages out beautiful women every day. You knew that when you started. And just maybe it would feel better than screwing a rich man in the hopes that he'll marry you and provide a dull future that will make you miserable." With an irritated-sounding huff, Cash pushed himself to the edge of the bed and stood.

Chrystal watched his lean, sexy body until he entered the primary bathroom. His bed felt cold without him in it.

Chapter Twenty-Nine

Rheagan ran the brush through her long auburn hair. She had spent extra time with the round brush, and her long hair was smooth and full. She and Greg had agreed to bring only casual clothes for their short trip, so she was wearing her favorite cream-colored sweater with pretty pearl buttons over snug jeans and ankle boots. She hoped her favorite sweater would bring her luck, and they would learn why Mike had kept secrets.

She tapped on Greg's door and didn't have long to wait before he opened it. He grinned at her in that sexy way that always deepened the laugh lines around his eyes. *Yup, there goes that electricity again …* Her lips reflexively turned up in a return smile, and he reached for her hand, continuing to hold it as they walked toward the elevators.

Downstairs, their Uber was waiting to take them to Michelangelo's Ristorante. They had agreed that Rheagan had a more sympathetic relationship with Mike, so the inquiries should come from her. They had also decided to enjoy the dinner first and ask their questions on the way out.

Rheagan saw the red-striped awning above the restaurant's windows as their Uber approached. It didn't appear as if the restaurant's façade had changed since the picture had been taken. She realized that she was holding her breath and forced herself to relax as Greg extended his hand and helped her out of the car.

Inside the restaurant, the atmosphere was dimly lit. She could see a dark walnut bar to the right, along with tables with red leather banquettes and white tablecloths. They checked in with the hostess, who took their coats and led them to their seats, handing each of them a menu. Opening it, Rheagan sighed in anticipation. "My dad would love this place. He adores old-school southern Italian, and this is that."

Their waiter came by to offer them drinks, and Greg ordered a nice bottle of Brunello. When they each had a glass in front of them, Greg raised his glass in a toast. As Rheagan raised her own, she wished there weren't so many secrets swirling around the two of them. As if he could read her mind, he said, "Here's to finding the answers we need."

They decided to order too many items and fully enjoy authentic Italian food in a city known for its Italian cuisine. They shared meatballs and bruschetta. Rheagan ordered the spaghetti carbonara, and Greg, the veal parmesan. They finished the bottle of wine, and as Greg settled the bill, he asked the waiter whether the man at the door was the owner, and was reassured that, indeed, Franco was.

Rheagan approached the older man. He had appeared earlier in the evening and was standing near the front door, greeting guests as they arrived. He smiled graciously at Rheagan as she neared him.

"Ciao," he said in greeting, "Did you enjoy your dinner?" His voice was deeply accented.

"Yes, very much, it was delicious," Rheagan assured him. She found herself suddenly nervous to ask him about the picture—there was a ridiculously low chance that he would recognize the young girl, and she would be wasting both their time. Still, she had come all the way here, and she owed Mike this much. She cleared her voice slightly. "Sir, forgive me, I recently lost my fiancé, Michael Carlucci, in an accident. I found this picture among his things. I wondered if you might know this young girl. It appears she is in front of your restaurant. Her name might have been Anna," she finished hurriedly.

Franco took the picture from her and studied it closely. Handing it back to her, he shook his head. "No, I'm sorry, the young girl does not look familiar to me. You must understand that we receive a large number of tourists, as well as our regular customers. I am sure I would remember a face as pretty as this," he said, handing the photo back to Rheagan with a smile. "And now, may I get your coats for you?" he offered as Greg joined them.

He disappeared into the back, and Greg squeezed her arm reassuringly, assuming from the short discussion that she had not gotten any helpful information. Franco reappeared with their coats, and they thanked him as they stepped out onto the sidewalk.

The evening was cool, but the fresh air felt good, and Rheagan breathed in deeply. Greg turned to her, pulling her against him in a big hug, and his eyes searched out hers. "He didn't recognize the girl in the photo?"

"No, he didn't recognize her."

"Are you okay?"

"I am. We knew this could happen. I just really thought we had a chance."

"Do you want to walk for a little bit? The streets are crowded, and we can stroll toward the hotel and eventually grab an Uber?"

"That sounds good," Rheagan agreed, looking forward to the chance of walking off the heavy meal and clearing her mind.

Greg reached for her hand and held it as they walked past other bustling Italian restaurants and closed-up Italian delis and specialty stores. Even through her disappointment, she felt the buzzing electricity of his touch. They had walked no more than three blocks when raindrops began to land on them. They lunged for a storefront awning as the skies opened and rain fell in sheets. Greg pulled Rheagan in tightly, and they huddled together in the protection of the closed store's entryway. Greg looked down at her and laughed. "I guess this would be a good time to call for that Uber?"

Rheagan raised her head to respond, and she saw his expression change from laughter to an intense focus on her lips, and she knew he was going to kiss her. *I should stop this …* His lips were firm and warm, and he tasted of expensive wine. He was holding her shoulders, and without even being aware, her arms found their way up to encircle his neck, deepening the kiss. He pulled her body in even closer, and the heat and maleness of that kiss was everything she had imagined. She felt that delicious electricity, and then the damning weight of Chrystal's secret.

She pulled back, and he immediately let her, retaining only a light touch on her shoulders as he looked questioningly into her eyes. "Greg, I shouldn't have let that happen," Rheagan said quietly and then, in a rush, she added, "I don't want to keep Chrystal's secret … She told me that night at the pub that she is pregnant with your child."

He stiffened, and she saw the flare of surprise in his eyes. He kissed her forehead gently before releasing her and then reached for his phone. "Let's get that Uber, and then are you up for a drink at the hotel? I want to talk to you about this."

"Of course," Rheagan responded. Greg took her hand and kept holding it until the Uber dropped them off at their hotel. His touch was a confusing mix of comfort and electricity.

They took the elevator to the lounge on the sixtieth floor, and Rheagan couldn't help but gasp in awe at seeing the view in the dark. Greg smiled down at her and said, "I like how you express pleasure in so many random things."

"Really?"

"Yeah, really," Greg said, leading her in the direction of a bar table in the corner of the room near the window. "Just in the last few days, it was appreciating the pink blanket, the view up here during the day, the bread at Parc, the butter at Parc ... should I go on? I am serious when I tell you, I like that about you ... You are joyful, and it's contagious."

She smiled at him and decided to be honest. "I also liked the kiss," she said.

"Ah, yes, I did too. Very much."

A waiter came over, and they each ordered a glass of red Burgundy. They made small talk and enjoyed the view of the twinkling city lights until the waiter brought them their wine, along with a bowl of mixed nuts and departed. Rheagan took a sip and then said, "I was in the ladies' room at Jack's pub, the Sunday you saw me with Kate, Jeff, and Sam."

Greg leaned forward, his face serious.

"Chrystal came in and blurted out that she was excited because she had just taken a pregnancy test and it was positive. She said that she just had to tell someone, but she didn't want to tell you yet because it was too soon. She asked me to keep her secret, and, Greg, I didn't want to—I just wasn't sure what to do."

Greg nodded. "Rheagan, you don't need to apologize. I'm struggling to understand her interaction with you, because it doesn't sound like Chrystal's style. Not to mention that we have never discussed a future together or starting a family. The irony is that I had intended to break things off with her that evening, but she told me that she was being phased out of her runway modeling work and asked me to attend her last show. I felt obligated to support her with that."

Greg took a sip of wine and reached out to touch Rheagan's arm. "In any case, I apologize for kissing you before things were completely over with Chrystal. I shouldn't have done that." He took a deep breath. "Rheagan, I have feelings for you, and I just reacted."

Rheagan felt a rush of joy followed by a reality check. He was still in a relationship with Chrystal, and the other woman was pregnant. *And how might Greg's feelings for me change if he knew that I had questioned my future with Mike?* She set her wine glass down and said, "Greg, I have feelings for you, too. Is that unfair to Mike?" She paused for a moment, glancing out the window and then added, "I understand you need to work through the issues with Chrystal. Mike's secrets have left me unsettled, too," she admitted, meeting his gaze.

Greg squeezed her shoulder. "Rheagan, Mike loved you deeply. I can't tell you what's behind the secrets, but I am sure that he loved you. We may have met because of Mike, but maybe the connection that we feel now is just about us. We both loved Mike, and having feelings for each other now doesn't change that."

Rheagan nodded and brushed a tear from her eye. "Thank you, I'm glad he had both of us." She finished her drink and set the glass down.

"And even though we have some complications, we can work through this," Greg said, looking deeply into her eyes.

"Greg, I … thank you, really." Rheagan smiled and met his gaze, her eyes soft.

Greg stifled a yawn. "We do have an early flight tomorrow. Are you ready to head to our rooms?"

"Sure," Rheagan said, grabbing her coat from the back of the chair as she stood. She reached into the zippered pocket to remove her room key, and a piece of paper fluttered to the floor. She bent down to pick it up and read the scrawled handwriting. "*You should go home and leave the past alone. That picture can bring nothing but trouble.*" She felt lightheaded and sat down abruptly.

"Rheagan, honey, are you okay?" Greg moved to her chair and bent down to look at her. She handed him the note, and he scanned it.

His expression went blank. He pulled her to her feet and toward the elevators.

Chapter Thirty

Greg took the card key from Rheagan's shaking grasp and opened her door. She walked inside, and he followed her. "This was undoubtedly Franco warning you to back off. Rheagan, I am so sorry now that I let you be the face of all this." He reached for her, holding her tightly. He felt a need to protect her and keep her safe.

"Hush," she said, reaching up to cup his face. "Mike was my fiancé, and I wanted to follow these leads. I needed to do it for me, Greg."

Later, he wouldn't be sure who made the first move, but then his arms were around her waist, and her arms were around his neck, pulling his lips closer to hers. The kiss was both fierce and tender, now that they had both shared their feelings for each other. His hands greedily brought her sexy body closer to him, and she responded with a soft moan of desire. Everything about her was authentic, and Greg had never wanted a woman more.

He laid her down on the bed and took his time with the buttons on her sweater, pressing soft kisses on each newly exposed area of skin. She was exquisitely soft and surprisingly curvy, despite her slender frame. He was lost in the delicate scent of her subtle floral fragrance and that soft silkiness of her long auburn hair, spilling all around them. He pushed the lacy cup of her bra aside and managed to capture her nipple in his lips, pulling and sucking at it while she moaned and pushed her breasts closer to his lips.

And then, as quickly as they could, they removed their remaining clothes and reveled in the feel of skin on skin and lips on skin. He rose to kiss her tenderly now, pushing back her hair to look into her eyes. They were passion-filled, but still she focused directly back at his own eyes as if to say, *I'm here with you.* Even so, he needed to hear it—he needed to know that Mike and Chrystal were not in the room. As if she could read his mind, she reached her hand up to his cheek and said, "I want you, Greg, I need to feel you, please …" As he filled her and felt the warmth and softness of her, he knew she was absolutely what he had been searching for. Later, as he was drifting off to sleep, he held her body close and wished the night would last forever.

Chapter Thirty-One

Angelina locked the door to her run-down apartment, dropped her keys in her purse, and smoothed down the material of her skirt. The damn thing was riding up a little again—she needed to go on another diet. "Too many late-night Snickers bars … But if I can't drink, I need something," she grumbled. She glanced at her watch and sighed. She was going to be late again—the snotty bitch had already warned her about being on time. *Ugh …*

She pressed the elevator button, and when the doors creaked open, she stepped in. As the doors closed behind her, she froze. Memories flooded in, and with them came white-hot fear. She held her breath, trying to escape the scent of stale cigars and cheap cologne.

When the elevator opened into the lobby of her apartment building, Angelina glanced in both directions and then darted out, heading toward the exit. Pure adrenaline coursed through her veins. She considered taking her beat-up car for the fastest escape but figured that was too obvious. Instead, she chose the sidewalk, trying to blend in with the other pedestrians.

A taxi passed her, and Angelina raised an arm to flag it down, but then she noticed that it was already taken. She was turning away when she saw the taxi pull into a Hilton Hotel.

She hurried to the entrance and stood in the lobby, taking deep breaths and considering her next move. And then, like a signal from her daddy, she saw it—a CPA conference advertising continuing education credits on the mezzanine level. Angelina joined a group of people heading toward the escalator.

Outside the conference room, a harried blonde woman handling registrations was distracted. Angelina scribbled "Anna C." on a white nametag and pressed it onto her shirt. She wished she could enjoy the irony of being Anna again, but the fear was too great. Grabbing a doughnut and a black coffee, she found a seat as close to the crowded middle of the room as she could find. Anonymity was what she was going for, and the sugar and coffee would keep her energy up. She needed to think clearly—*Mike needs me not to mess this up.*

Chapter Thirty-Two

Greg opened his eyes as the plane was descending to land at Seattle-Tacoma International Airport. He looked over at Rheagan's sleeping profile, and, despite the lack of sleep and the unsettling situation they were in, he felt a strange sense of optimism. She had the pink blanket pulled up to her chin, but one of her hands was outside the blanket and tucked securely into his.

Memories of being in bed with Rheagan the night before filled his heart, but his thoughts were spinning. They had spent much of the rest of the night talking about the note and what it might mean. The irony was that visiting Michelangelo's Ristorante had been their last clue to follow. *By taking that step, which turned up nothing, have we now put ourselves in some unknown danger?* Greg had his fears, but he wanted to shield Rheagan as much as possible until they knew more. He looked at her sleeping profile and promised himself that he would protect her.

In addition to Mike's past, he had his own Chrystal bombshell to deal with. The night before, Rheagan and Greg had agreed that he needed to resolve his issues before they could take things further, and he very much wanted to do so. During the flight, he'd used the plane's Wi-Fi to contact a private investigator he had worked with on various business cases. He had decided to have Chrystal followed, since Sam had seen her with another man. He wasn't sure that he even believed she was pregnant, but in any case, information was always helpful. The landing announcement came on over the intercom, and Greg turned to see Rheagan open those beautiful caramel eyes and smile at him.

From the airport, they took an Uber to Lake Washington, where they boarded the seaplane that would take them to Whisper Island. After deplaning, Greg drove her back to her building, and they walked up the stairs to her unit.

When Rheagan opened the door, he could hear Mr. Pickle's energetic approach to greet them. She bent down to pick up the purring cat, and Greg reached over to give him a scratch under his chin. As they walked into the kitchen, Rheagan pointed to a new cat toy on the floor. "Mr. Pickles is getting spoiled—first you, and now Kate's apparently given him a new toy."

She set the squirming feline down and turned to Greg. "Do we really need to do this?" she asked.

"Yes, honey," he said, squeezing her shoulder and meeting her eyes. "I'm sorry for the inconvenience, but I feel like it's necessary until we know more. If there's any chance someone cares enough about that photo to come looking for it … well, I want to be sure they run into a dead end with you. Your safety means everything to me."

She nodded, opened a drawer, and removed Mike's latest cell phone, handing it to Greg along with the envelope from the safe-deposit box. She opened the door to the hall, and he followed her to her office, where she disconnected her laptop. Grabbing a box from the closet that held Mike's laptop, she laid hers on top.

"Honey, I want the printer too. Remember, you uploaded and printed the photo of Anna in front of the restaurant. Printers have memory too. And I'm going to need your cell phone."

Rheagan let out an audible sigh of frustration, but she still managed to give him a sweet smile. "I know you are doing this to help keep me safe, but ugh … This is a lot of work."

"I know, and I'm very sorry, but I think it's necessary. I will hold all of this in my office safe and will return it to you as soon as possible. Rheagan, thank you for not fighting me on this. I wish we had thought this through better, but we let you be the face of our fact-finding mission."

She nodded, and he reached for her, wrapping his arms around her. He had meant the hug to be about comfort, but the minute she was in his arms, he sensed that they both were feeling a pull of attraction. "Everything we ordered to replace this computer equipment should be here tomorrow, and your burner phone should be delivered by this evening," Greg said, trying to break the spell. He looked down into her eyes to be certain she was comfortable with the timing. He wanted to move fast on this. "I know you'll miss having this phone with all your stuff on it, but the burner phone is just for a few weeks, to be sure nothing comes of that warning from Franco."

"Tomorrow I will be hating life, getting logged into all my accounts, but I get it. Oh, and heads-up on Mike's old phone. I still haven't been able to get into it. I sent the phone company the documentation, and I'm waiting for their response. Should I reach out to them again and see where things stand?"

Greg paused. "Yes, let's do that right now on your phone before I take it, and then don't contact them again. Based on what they tell you, we can retrieve your phone from my safe and monitor the progress. Hopefully, we'll get access soon. Remember … after today, do not use any of your new electronics for anything related to Mike. Promise me that, Rheagan."

"I promise," Rheagan said, meeting his concerned eyes and reaching for the phone he handed her.

Chapter Thirty-Three

Greg planned to call Chrystal while he was in Seattle to see a client. He had decided to use the impromptu business meeting as an excuse to visit her. He wanted to catch her off guard when he confronted her about her pregnancy news. She had been acting out of character lately—that much he had noted several times. *Maybe because of the pregnancy … Or is it that she's seeing another man?* He didn't feel good about letting this situation go. With Chrystal's pregnancy, the two of them had some decisions to make. He dialed her number and waited for her to pick up.

She answered on the third ring and sounded irritable. "Hey, how was Philadelphia?"

"It was a couple of long days. How are you?"

"I'm good, I guess. I don't think we've been seeing enough of each other recently," she griped, her tone making it clear who was to blame for that situation.

"Well, then, you might be happy to know that I'm in your neighborhood. I had an unexpected meeting to attend. Any chance I can drop by now?"

There was a pause. "Sure, I just got back from the gym, but come on over." Her tone lacked its usual breathiness.

"See you shortly," Greg replied, disconnecting. He smiled as he put the phone in his pocket. For whatever reason, Chrystal was not excited about him dropping by, which increased his chances of having a more honest conversation with her.

She buzzed him into the building and opened her front door at his knock. She was dressed in a loose, silky black robe, full makeup, and a lousy attitude.

Let's get this over with. He hadn't kissed her, and he wasn't even sure she had noticed. She led him into her living room and offered him a beverage, which he declined.

She seemed to gather herself then and said, "I'm sorry, babe, I just wasn't expecting you, but it's a nice surprise."

The lack of sincerity in her tone was palpable, and Greg found himself, once again, so tired of her personas. *Do I even really know this woman?* "I understand you're pregnant."

Her jaw tensed, and her eyes went flat, but the expression on her face didn't change. "So, she told you. I asked her not to, as we are still in the early stages."

"I think she felt uncomfortable knowing personal information about me. The more interesting issue is why you would share the information with her rather than with me?"

Her voice softened. "Oh, Greg, don't be frustrated with me … not about this … I wanted to give it a little more time to be completely certain and then share it with you in a special moment. I want you to be happy about our baby."

"We haven't talked about a future or about having children together. The last conversation I recall relating in any way to this was ensuring that we were using protection." Greg fought to keep his tone wry rather than accusatory.

Chrystal smiled apologetically. “I guess birth control isn’t one hundred percent effective, and maybe the timing works out after all, since I won’t be doing runway shows anymore.” Her voice grew softer, and her eyes were downcast.

“Chrystal, how far along are you?”

“The doctor estimates eleven weeks.”

Greg nodded, trying to keep his expression even, but he felt sick. “So, you’ve been to see a doctor?”

“Yes, I wanted to know for sure.”

Greg paused, trying to meet her eyes, but she was looking down at her stomach, gently rubbing it. “Chrystal, we are going to need to talk about this. Before this news, I didn’t see a future for us. This pregnancy doesn’t change that.”

She lifted her head, and he saw that, despite his comment, her eyes held an expression of unexpected confidence. “Greg, this is why I wanted to be the one to tell you, and under different circumstances.” She stood up, moved into the kitchen, and came back holding a paper, which she handed to him. He could see the ultrasound, and he felt crushing disappointment.

Oblivious, she moved closer. “We are good together, Greg. We’ve been seeing each other for at least a year. We just need to spend more time together …” She untied her robe, and it fell open to reveal her totally naked body. She reached for his hand to pull him to his feet.

He allowed her to pull him up, but when he stood, he lifted her chin, forcing her eyes to meet his. “I’m not staying, Chrystal. I need time to think about how we handle this.” He walked to her front door and looked back. She had followed him out to the hall, her robe was still open, and she had a triumphant gleam in her eyes.

Greg shut her door behind him, shaking his head. *That's the only card she knows to play.* He had the clear realization that spending the night with Rheagan had felt right, and taking advantage of what Chrystal had just offered would have felt like cheating.

Chapter Thirty-Four

Rheagan hit *Print* and smiled as she heard the sound of gratifying success. She was a reasonably techie person, but this week had been brutal. Installing and logging into all the necessary programs for her finance and provisioning functions had been a hugely frustrating expenditure of her time. She had also struggled to explain to her parents why she had a new phone number, but figured that telling them the truth was a non-starter.

Despite the technology headaches, her work with Joe on updating the menus for Savor was progressing at a satisfying clip. This week, they were featuring veal scallopini with mushrooms, which was delicious and a hit with the guests. She and Joe had even discussed pizzas, but Rheagan felt that would require adding a dedicated oven. They had pizzas on the family meal rotation now and continued to work on new flavor combinations, but they weren't her priority.

In the afternoon, she was meeting with Greg to review the contents of Mike's phone. After following up with the phone company, the two had been referred to Apple for access to the data stored on the phone and backed up in the cloud. They had sent the requested legal information to the manufacturer and had been told to expect access to the information today. Greg had cautioned her that they might still not find any answers related to Mike's past, but at least she could retrieve pictures and store them temporarily on her old laptop.

It was a Thursday, so she was going to head over to Greg's office around 4:00 and then return to the restaurant for dinner service. She had kept looking at her watch all day, anxious to find out what Mike's old phone held—plus Greg had told her that he was going to see Chrystal this week. *I wonder how that went.* She reminded herself that Chrystal had more right to be with him right now, but that didn't make her any less impatient to hear how the discussion had gone. *She's having his baby, so what does that mean for his future?*

She dressed carefully for their meeting. Sure, she had to dress for her front-of-house duties at Savor afterwards, but she knew she was taking extra care with her hair and makeup. Promptly at 4:00 p.m., Nan ushered her into Greg's office, and Rheagan felt a purely feminine reaction to the way that Greg's eyes went directly to her legs in her black pencil skirt. She wondered if Nan could feel the heightened tension between her and Greg.

When Nan left them, Greg took her hands and pulled her in for a gentle, sexy hug that set her insides tingling. "Are you ready for this?"

"I am," Rheagan said, aware of her anxiety.

Greg handed her the phone, and they followed the instructions provided. The phone turned on, but without the screensaver—a picture of her from culinary school—that Rheagan was used to seeing. She tapped on the photos icon and quickly scanned the albums. Then, puzzled, she turned to him. "Greg, there are a lot of pictures missing."

"Can you categorize them for me? Are older photos missing, perhaps, or photos he might have saved by "occasion? Maybe some pictures were only saved in the cloud?"

Rheagan scrolled through the list of albums and then turned back to Greg. She could hear the bewilderment in her own voice. "The missing pictures are of us, Greg. There are no pictures of you or me on his phone."

"Okay, I have a contact name and number from Apple. Why don't you go on to work, and I will see if I can figure out this mystery. So just to be clear, this is not how you remember his phone?"

"No, I know—he had a ton of pictures of us." She felt the anxiety building again. She opened the email icon and said, "Greg, there are no emails from us, either."

"Now that we've inserted me into the process as your attorney, I'll make a call and let you know what I find out. Don't worry, Rheagan, we'll get those pictures back. Go on to Savor, and I will text you." He gave her a tight hug, and she felt that support from him again. *How would I have made it through all this without him?*

A little after 7:00, Rheagan checked her phone and saw a message from Greg.

GREG: Got some answers, will catch up with you soon.

Rheagan wasn't exactly sure how to interpret his message but figured he was telling her not to worry. It didn't work. *Just breathe and focus on the things here at Savor.* By 8:30, her last customers had left, and she was busy with the closing process when her phone chimed.

GREG: Any chance I can stop by and see you in a bit?

Her stomach clenched, even as her fingers typed.

RHEAGAN: Absolutely. Meet you at the Savor entrance.

In a few short minutes, she heard his tap at the door, and she opened it to let him in. He smiled reassuringly at her as she guided him over to a table. He took the seat she offered, and when she sat down too, he said, "No, Rheagan, please finish up what you need to do. I can wait."

"Greg, it's late. This can't be good." Her words tumbled out, and he reached forward, grabbing her hand and squeezing it.

"It's just more information, Rheagan. I'll hang out until you're done."

"Can I get you a drink? Red?"

"Sure," he said with another reassuring smile.

Her head wasn't in the game as she finished up, but luckily for her, she had closed a restaurant more times than she could count. *I know he seems calm, but Greg wouldn't be here at 9:00 p.m. on a Thursday if he had good news.* After what seemed much longer than twenty minutes, she wrapped up and walked back to the kitchen to say goodnight to Joe and the staff.

Chapter Thirty-Five

Angelina tried to calm her roiling mind. *I have to focus.* This all-day seminar was providing her with precious time to plan her next steps. She knew she had not overreacted. They were looking for her—correction, they had found her. But why? After all these years, why? For God's sake, she hadn't even testified. That fact alone had to have made it clear to them that she didn't have enough for the Feds. *Next steps … next steps, I don't have time to think about why.*

She only had an ID under her real name, Angelina Bonasera. She didn't dare use it. She would withdraw as much cash as possible from the hotel's ATM on her way out. She needed to use cash from now on and leave no trail. Going back to her apartment or renting a hotel room using her ID was impossible. She needed a seedy day-rental. She began searching for options on her phone. Was it even safe to use her phone? Could they track her location using cell tower data? Did they have those connections in Los Angeles? She forced her fear aside. She didn't have a choice—she had to find her next place.

At lunch, she managed to stuff a spare half sandwich into her purse. At the end of the day, she filed out with the certified public accountants, even though she wanted nothing more than to remain in the sanctuary of that conference room. As she passed the registration desk, the blonde woman sitting there thanked her for attending.

Downstairs, she rushed to the ATM, withdrew the maximum allowed amount, $500, and headed to the taxi stand, keeping her head down. She had the taxi drop her off at a Walmart, where she purchased a blonde wig, a sweatshirt, matching sweatpants, socks, sneakers, scissors, several boxes of crackers, and a couple of cans of beans with pull-tab lids. She wanted desperately to buy cigarettes, but if she hadn't been able to afford them before, money had instantly become even tighter. On foot now, she carried her purchases to the seedy hotel she had selected earlier. When she opened the front door, the smell of mildew and desperation enveloped her. *Welcome to the Duchess Hotel.*

Chapter Thirty-Six

Greg followed Rheagan to her apartment, where Mr. Pickles waited inside the door. She led him to her cozy kitchen and reached for a bottle of red wine. After pouring two generous glasses, she turned to him, and he could see a combination of fear and sadness in her questioning expression.

Greg cleared his throat. "I spoke to the rep from Apple. They told me that Mike performed a large deletion of pictures and data from his iCloud account. He followed that up by deleting his 'Recently Deleted File.' Unfortunately, the result of those two steps renders that data typically unrecoverable." Greg had reached out to hold Rheagan's hand, and he continued to hold it as she processed the information in shocked silence.

"What does any of this mean?" Her words came out slowly, and they sounded monotone to him. She let go of his hand, reached down for Mr. Pickles, and, holding him tightly to her, just looked off into the distance. Greg wished he had answers to give her. But for now, all he had were his suspicions, and he didn't like them.

"Rheagan, I don't know anything for sure, but let me share what I've been considering. Mike was close to only a few people in his life. He kept secrets even from those folks. For God's sake, we were warned off at an Italian restaurant. I'm thinking it's a possibility that Mike and/or his mother may have been in the Witness Protection Program."

Rheagan's eyes filled with tears, and Greg knew those tears were for what Mike must have gone through. "That's why you wanted all of my electronics … In case there were people from his past who may have wanted to harm him or Anna. Do you think that's why I didn't find any personal mementos in our house and why he deleted all the pictures?" Rheagan's face was pale as her words tumbled out, and he thought she might be shaking.

He reached for her arm and held it. "Again, these are just guesses, but we know Mike did take pictures of us—we've both seen them over the years. So yes, I think something happened to concern Mike, and he deleted our pictures."

"Oh my God," Rheagan said on a sob. The startled Mr. Pickles jumped from her lap, and Greg pulled her into his arms. He held her while the sobs shook her slender body, and eventually, she pushed herself back, reaching for a napkin to wipe her eyes and nose.

"I have to believe," Greg continued, "and I've given this a lot of thought, that he didn't consider you to be in physical danger. I think he was doing everything he could think of to keep you safe."

"Do we know when he deleted everything?" Rheagan asked, her voice so faint that he could barely hear her.

"No, Apple won't share that without additional clearance. Just guessing, though, it might have been when he said he lost his phone."

Suddenly, Rheagan's expression turned intense. "Greg, what if Mike's accident wasn't just an accident?"

Greg nodded and said, “I thought of that too, honey, but it doesn't seem likely. I reviewed the police report and spoke with the officers who interviewed the driver and conducted the investigation. It seems to have been a legitimate accident. I'm not well-versed in mob hits, but I find it hard to imagine they could orchestrate an accident like the one that took Mike's life.”

Rheagan nodded, but her face remained pale, and she took a long swallow of her wine. “So, if something happened to scare Mike, we don't know what it was, but we don't feel like it caused his death.”

“Yes, honey, that about sums it up.”

“What, if anything, should we do about this?”

“I think we should talk to the police tomorrow. They may not tell us anything—they may not even know anything. I don't think local police are necessarily notified if someone in the program moves into their town. But we can ask them to keep an eye on your place.”

Rheagan nodded her head and took another sip of wine. “Okay, that sounds like a plan.” Her lips turned up into a wry smile, but her eyes just looked tired and sad.

“Can I spend the night on your couch tonight? I would feel better if I didn't leave you. I just shared some unsettling news, and I don't want you to be anxious and by yourself.” Greg's eyes caught on hers. “I promise I will stay on the couch.”

She managed a trembling smile, but she shook her head. “Thank you, Greg, but nothing happened this evening other than that we have more information.”

“Still, I really don't want to leave you alone right now. Please let me stay?”

She smiled sadly and shook her head again. "Greg, I'm just so sad, but I can't allow myself to start feeling afraid in my own home."

He pulled her in for a long, gentle hug and just held her. Finally, she broke away and said, "Do you mind if I take off my makeup and come back out to share another glass of wine with you … Maybe I'm not ready to be alone just yet?"

"Of course, honey. Go do your thing, and I'll get the wine and be waiting for you here."

Greg was sipping a Cabernet Sauvignon when Rheagan came back. She was wearing a pair of leggings and an oversized T-shirt that read "Culinary Institute of America." Her long hair was in that messy bun thing again, and her face was bare of makeup. She joined him on the couch and accepted the glass of wine he handed her.

"I like to see you without makeup. I can see your freckles better."

Rheagan managed a slight smile. "It's that Irish peeking out again." She took a sip of wine, and then her eyes turned serious. "How did you and Mike become such close friends? In many ways, the two of you seem very different."

Greg nodded. "Maybe it was perfect timing that we met when both of us were in transition. We were placed as roommates our first year at UW. I was supposed to have my own room, but at the last minute, the school notified us that, at least temporarily, they needed to place a new student in my room. Mike and I were very different, but we clicked right away and had something to offer each other. The bond we built lasted.

"On my end, despite growing up with the Andersen-Karlsson name and all that comes with it, I had lived a pretty sheltered life. Everyone I'd grown up with and interacted with on a day-to-day basis was aware of my situation. In most cases, we had known each other all our lives. My father, while intellectually brilliant, was a laid-back, former hippie type from Whisper Island, and he didn't even think to prepare me for meeting opportunistic and self-serving individuals. Had my mother still been alive, she would have played that role. She had come from a very wealthy, uptight background and would have known the landscape."

Greg took a sip of his wine, and his face formed a cynical smile. "It eventually became evident to me that some instructors treated me with a level of deference, and that some enterprising and ambitious students had actually researched that I would be attending school at UW and made a point of introducing themselves to me. Whether those students were male or female, they each had their own unique agenda. Mike caught on to this well before I did, and he taught me how to limit access and basically protect myself. To this day, I still follow his advice of leaving off the hyphenated Karlsson from my last name so I can blend in better." He laughed. "When he came to visit me here on Whisper Island, I had to assure him that Sam and Kate were not like the others.

"And I guess, my gift to him in return was a family. Mike was always private, but my father accepted others and welcomed their eccentricities because he had his own. He never pried into why Mike was on his own in the world—he just welcomed him unconditionally. My dad was terrific, and I give him credit for perhaps seeing even more than I did—that Mike needed stability. And what about you? Tell me about meeting Mike."

She reached forward and pulled Mr. Pickles onto her lap with a pensive expression on her face. "I first became aware of a buzz around Mike's ability to master complex cooking techniques. If there was a challenging class or process, say for instance, executing a clear consommé, he was the student to talk to. He wasn't particularly friendly, but neither was he unfriendly. We took a baking class together, and since most of the course was very scientific and precise, given that it was baking, he excelled. However, our instructor threw us a curve one day by introducing creativity and asking us to develop a new and surprising flavor combination. It was the first time I had seen Mike unsure of his next steps." Rheagan smiled. "You can imagine how irritable Mike got with any level of uncertainty. He noticed I was working away and came over to see what I was doing. I think he liked my confidence but absolutely hated my ingredient. I was adding cilantro to something. Anyway, soon after, and despite the hated cilantro, our relationship became personal."

Greg smiled gently. "I was intrigued when he told me about you. I could tell it was different. Mike never had difficulty finding women to be with—he just never wanted any commitment before you. He told me that he had never expected to find someone like you. He called you his 'lighthouse.' He said you were strong and that he could count on you."

Greg noticed Rheagan brushing tears from her eyes, and her hand shook as she reached for her wine glass. *I still feel like she's keeping something from me … but maybe I'm just feeling guilty because I haven't told her that Chrystal showed me an ultrasound picture.*

Chapter Thirty-Seven

Sheriff Jansen's tired blue eyes and lined face showed little expression as Greg laid out their facts and suspicions. But when he finished speaking, the sheriff favored them both with a stern yet sympathetic look. "I am sorry for the uncertainty and concerns that have, no doubt, stirred up painful feelings for you both. However," he added as he spread his bony hands across his shiny desk, "I need you to leave any future investigative activities to my department."

Greg and Rheagan both nodded, and the sheriff continued, "Greg, you are correct that my department has not received any communication from WITSEC, the witness protection organization, regarding Mike. I can also inform you that even if my office were to contact WITSEC, they likely would not disclose any information, not even to confirm or deny Mike's situation, based on the facts you have shared with me. What I can tell you, and it may give you comfort, is that if they are involved and discover credible evidence of a threat to you, they will reach out if they need our assistance, including eyes on the ground. I also want to assure you that, based on our thorough investigation, it is my full belief that Mike's death was nothing more than a tragic but random vehicle accident."

Again, Greg and Rheagan nodded.

"Lastly, I will provide additional patrol presence for your residences and businesses to ensure your security. Perhaps with no further investigation on your part, any interest, if there was any, will dissipate," he said pointedly, looking at them both.

The two of them managed to keep a measured expression until they had walked a reasonable distance from the Whisper Island sheriff's department. "So that felt exactly like being in the principal's office," Rheagan said, grinning.

Greg laughed without restraint. *Even in tough times, she provides levity.* "It was the classic, 'leave it to the professionals,' there's no questioning that." He reached over, grabbing her hand and squeezing it briefly before releasing it. "Do you have a few minutes? I wanted to update you on my conversation with Chrystal."

"I was curious but didn't want to pry," Rheagan said quietly.

"Rheagan, please don't feel like you're prying," Greg said, looking earnestly down at her. "I did see her briefly while I was in Seattle on Wednesday. Honey, she confirmed she is pregnant and said something similar to what she told you. She was waiting for a better moment to tell me." He shook his head. "Chrystal tends to play games, which is why I wanted to surprise her with both my visit and my knowledge of the pregnancy. She was upset that you told me and was not pleased when I confronted her. When I asked, she estimated that she is about eleven weeks pregnant." His voice softened, and he tilted his head, searching out her eyes. "She had an ultrasound picture of the baby."

He saw the flush of tears in Rheagan's eyes, and he pulled her close. "Rheagan, you've been through so much, and I don't want to add to that. I know my feelings for you are real. I've given this a lot of thought, and a future with Chrystal is impossible for me. Another wrinkle in this situation is that Sam recently shared that Mindy has seen Chrystal with another man a couple of times, and that things appeared intimate between them. I'm going to have a private investigator follow her briefly, and I will insert myself into her next doctor's appointments in the interim. Honey, I'm sorry—this could be messy. Do you want some space?"

Rheagan reached her arms up, pulling his head down so his lips met hers for a brief kiss. "Complications and all, I'm in, but let's give you some room to get the answers you need."

Greg nodded and leaned in for another kiss filled with promise. When he released her, he reached for her hand. "Rheagan, despite all the drama in our lives right now, I would love to spend Sunday with you. And … I've been thinking, did you ever review the search history or deleted files from Mike's laptop after his death? Maybe something there would give us more information?"

Rheagan shook her head. "No, it never occurred to me." Then she grinned up at him and asked, "So wait, does that mean we're continuing with our investigative activities?"

Greg laughed and caught her up in a bear hug.

Chapter Thirty-Eight

Angelina looked at her reflection in the mirror, and Anna looked back at her. She hated Anna, and looking like her again made a very bad situation even worse. She had enjoyed having her hair dark again and letting it grow. She had enjoyed dressing up a little for work and had even considered trying to date again. Dating was hard, though … She only really liked the wrong guys, and that had gotten her and Mike pulled out of Minneapolis and stuck in that godforsaken, dreary SeaTac.

I don't want to think about the bad decisions I've made, she thought as she moved around the shoddy room. Honestly, there were just too many to count. *Maybe even this is a bad decision,* she realized, taking a sip of the rot-gut gin that she had gone out to purchase after transforming back into Anna. *But drinking too much is a very Anna thing to do.*

Focus … focus … It was too late for Daddy, and it was too late for her, but she needed to save Mike. She felt the wet track of tears on her face. By now, Dom had likely been in her apartment and gone through all her things. That meant they had her computer. She had tried to erase it, but they were smarter than her. She should have gotten rid of it, but hadn't had the money to buy a new one.

So, they probably knew that she had contacted Mike. Even through the numbness caused by the gin, she felt a pang of guilt. She'd known better. Agent Barrett had told her never to put Mike in danger. All she'd done was search for his name and seen the article. She had been so proud of him—her son starting a restaurant. She had just reached out that one time to let him know that …

Focus … focus … but her system wasn't used to the gin, and she couldn't think very clearly. Her eyes started to drift shut, and she forced them open. *My phone is all the way across the room—I'll close my eyes for a minute … No, I can't let Mike down.*

With the phone in her hand, she collapsed on the bed, waiting for the room to stop spinning before she typed in "Michael Carlucci, Whisper Island." The search engine returned several results, and her eyes focused on the top entry. "Local chef killed when his bicycle collides with an automobile." Angelina closed her eyes and escaped into the blackness.

Chapter Thirty-Nine

Rheagan turned on the light in the *Inspiration Room* and moved toward the table with her cup of coffee. A rare gleam of morning sunlight bounced off the glass pane of the window, and Rheagan noticed a faint reflection of herself. The image she saw was of a stylish woman with a confident stride. She allowed herself to enjoy and acknowledge that she was that woman. She turned her attention to the organized yet colorful room and the healthy plants she regularly tended to. It felt good to be in here now—it even felt *inspiring*. She laid the almost-finished menu down on the table. The pieces were finally falling into place. It had been a lot of work. She and Joe had spent countless hours updating the recipes, tweaking them until they were satisfied. Then his team had to practice cooking them. Even the servers had to learn new descriptions and flavors; it was truly a team effort. Rheagan was proud of all of them and proud of herself. Joe was coming to join her in a few minutes, but first, she wanted to spend some time with Mike.

She focused on the CIA manual and felt that connection to him again, the same one that the book with his handwritten notes always evoked. *Oh, Mike, I loved you, and it hurts so bad to think about what you must have endured. How strong you must have been to survive. Mike, please forgive me for having doubts about us …*

Once Greg had shared his suspicions about Mike and Anna being involved in witness protection, everything had started to make more sense to her. The witness protection theory fit with what they had discovered since Mike's death, but most of all, it made sense to her, having shared a life with him. She anticipated the freedom of letting go of the last secret she had been keeping. When the time was right, she was ready to share her doubts about Mike with Greg, and she prayed that he would understand.

Joe walked in with his coffee in hand and sat across the table from her. "I say we do it, Chef. I've been thinking about the idea of homemade pasta, and I think we need to add it to the menu."

Rheagan smiled at Savor's new head chef. "I think we do too. Maybe we can start with just three pastas and see how it goes? A pasta entrée is also a good way to ensure we have vegetarian options on the menu, as well as a way to make swaps for vegans."

"Ah, good points. I'll be honest with you—I made pasta in culinary school but haven't done it much since."

"Not a problem, Joe. I can show you some tips, and I'll be pretty hands-on, especially in the beginning. Let's make it fresh in the mornings, but keep some on hand in the refrigerator from the day before, just in case. As with all the changes we're making, we will likely need to make adjustments once we have a longer track record of the dishes that are ordered regularly. I'm going to start looking for a good extruder machine."

"Also, Chef, just thought I'd mention that the Caesar salad is a popular item, and we are getting requests to serve the chicken cutlet from the Milanese salad on it. So that salad is acting as another entrée."

"Interesting ... that's good news. It is a really excellent salad, and that garlicky anchovy paste is delicious. Let's add it as an entrée. We have room on the menu." She smoothed her hand across their working draft. "Everything else going well? Is the team good?"

Joe cocked his head and paused for a moment. "I couldn't ask for a better sous chef than Trey. His skills are legit. Manny has stepped up tremendously, and it's fun to see his growth, but he gets that Trey earned the promotion, and he is focused on the details to improve himself." Joe lifted his coffee cup toward Rheagan and smiled. "The team is fired up. We are creating a bunch of *nonnas* down there."

Rheagan had just taken a sip of her own coffee and came close to spitting it out as she laughed.

It was Kate and Rheagan's regularly scheduled "Girls Night," and when Rheagan opened her front door, her friend's exuberant hug practically knocked her over.

"Jeff asked me to marry him!"

"Oh, Kate! That's wonderful! Let's see your ring!" Rheagan reached for the hand that Kate proudly thrust at her, and she smiled with delight at the shimmering, square-cut diamond. "Oh Kate, it's gorgeous, I'm so happy for you! She gave her friend a big hug and, still holding Kate's hand, she began pulling her toward the kitchen. "Let's celebrate!"

Kate settled into a chair at the kitchen island, still smiling widely as Rheagan pulled champagne out of the wine refrigerator. The bottle opened with a resounding pop, and, with an exaggerated flourish, Rheagan poured each of them a glass.

"He asked me last night. A total surprise. Flowers, candles ... You know, I think he was actually nervous. Not that I would turn him down, but just nervous because he wanted me to feel special. Oh, Rheagan, I feel so lucky to have found someone like him." Kate's brown eyes drifted back to her hand and the sparkling ring.

"Honey, he openly adores you. Here's to your happily ever after!" Rheagan raised her glass and tapped it against Kate's.

They each took a sip of the bubbly in their flutes, and then Kate's eyes turned mischievous. "Now spill the beans on you and Greg. I can feel the heat from a block away!"

"Ah ... There's heat, and it's complicated, but I feel lucky too. Whatever it ends up being, I'm glad to have him in my life right now. But this isn't the night to talk about me. I want to hear all the details. Start talking, girlfriend!"

Chapter Forty

Dom felt the weight of his years like a worn-out coat. His line of work was hard on a man's body. He drank a black coffee, trying to blend in with the other customers in the coffee shop. He didn't like doing work in different cities. And he didn't blend in well, he decided as he noticed a stare from a couple of young professionals.

He would be leaving Los Angeles soon; he had Angelina's laptop in his possession, and he was on his way to see her now. He shook his head—her apartment had been a mess. He couldn't imagine living like that. She had turned out to be such a disappointment. He finished his coffee and dumped the empty cup in the trash can. As he lumbered past, he gave the young professionals his best menacing stare, just for sport.

He followed the directions to the Duchess Hotel and smiled. He recognized the type—they existed in every city. No one here would ask any questions. He strolled in and went straight to the rickety elevator.

Her room was on the twentieth floor, but he doubted that it had a view of anything worth seeing. He reached her room and rattled the doorknob, smiling again. *Just one good push.* He slammed the door hard with his bad shoulder and was inside. He was unprepared for the smell of vomit and spilled gin.

"Jesus Christ," he grumbled, focusing on the woman curled in the corner.

As he studied her, she pushed herself up. She was heavier now and had god-awful, blonde, choppy hair. Her once lovely face was now only cheap and hard.

"Here," she said, coming closer to him with the phone in her hand.

He used his training to hold back any reaction to the smell of bile and cheap booze that wafted from her as she moved.

She appeared to be trying to find something on her phone. "This is what you came for," she said. "He's dead. You tell Luca I'll see him in hell."

Dom accepted the phone from her, read the brief headline, and turned his attention back to Angelina. She fixed him with a sullen glare and spoke, her words slurred. "We were in love, I know we were. He even gave me the most gorgeous ring. It was a silver rose with a ruby in the center." She started to cry. "Then you all had to go and ruin it!"

Dom felt the rush of anger overwhelm him. *It was Luca who took that ring … That goddamned ring, the one I got blamed for going missing."* The mob had stolen the ring during a hit on a judge and his girlfriend, who had been proudly wearing it in a press picture caught of them earlier in the night. Then, it went missing from both the crime scene and the mob's "Processing Room." *This could finally change everything for me.* He forced his attention back to Angelina. He needed more information, and, like it was yesterday, he remembered how to play her. "I didn' know, Lina. An' it went so bad for youz guys. That ring mus' be special … Why ain't ya wearin it? Do ya still have it or a picture to rememba?"

Angelina sniffed loudly and reached for the phone. Dom watched intently over her shoulder as she selected the Photos app and began searching. After a moment, she pulled up an old picture of her standing with Luca in front of Franco's restaurant, wearing that goddamned ring.

"Oh, I see it, yeah." Dom reached for the phone, and Angelina handed it back to him. Her tired, hard face wore a ridiculously coquettish and smug expression. The minute he secured the phone, he tapped on the photo, shared it to her text app, added his phone number, and hit the phone icon. The look on her face morphed immediately into suspicion. "Hey, why do you care about that ring? It was between me and Luca." She reached for her phone.

Dom held it out of her reach and advanced on her. "Where'z the ring now?"

"That ring was nothing, Dom—he married Susan anyway." She was arguing with him, but her voice was filled with fear.

"I want the goddamned ring." Dom heard his own voice, quiet and mean.

Angelina began backing away, her expression a mix of fear and resignation. Too late, he realized the window behind her was open. He reached for her, but she was too far away, and as he lunged, she threw herself forward and through the opening.

Dom cursed and limped to the window. When he looked down, the broken body of the woman he had once loved lay on the sidewalk below. He slipped her phone into his pocket and quickly searched the room before someone arrived to investigate Angelina's fall. *Where is that goddamned ring?* He didn't have long to look, but he figured if she'd still had it, she would likely have been wearing it. He moved toward the door. It was time to go home.

Chapter Forty-One

Dom deactivated the alarm system and entered the house from the back door. He had suggested that Luca might want to have the house emptied of his wife and servants due to the sensitivity of the information he had to share. He plodded to the study and took his usual chair, waiting for Luca to arrive. He was generally a patient man—it paid to be in his business.

Probably thirty minutes later, he heard Luca's arrival and the security sweep by his agent. Finally, he heard Luca coming toward him. Dom had used the time while he waited to figure out how best to handle the situation. Because it wasn't just the thirty minutes he had been waiting. He had been waiting for this since he was still a teenager. He had always hated Luca. *He is nothing but a pretty boy who thought he was too good to do the jobs that the rest of us did.* And stealing Angelina, well, Dom had long ago decided that he'd gotten the better end of that deal. But the ring business, that was unforgivable and disloyal to all they stood for. The hit on the judge had been Dom's job and the one and only time Luca had been included in a "job." That well-publicized ring gone missing had cost him, Dom, personally. You don't take souvenirs from a job. He was certain that single event had deprived him of his well-deserved status as a "made man" in the family.

Luca stalked into the room, filled with his personal brand of irritation and self-importance, but Dom remained silent and motionless, robbing the other man of any reaction.

Luca poured himself a scotch, neat, and took his seat behind the desk. "Well, what did you find?" he asked in his arrogant tone, taking a long sip of his scotch.

"We found ya to be a disappointment an' a risk. It turns out I was right, the boss, he don' like secrets. Wittout trust, he got no use for ya."

Luca sat up straight in his chair, and the look on his finely chiseled face was one of utter shock. On anyone else, Dom might have found the look and the situation amusing. But with Luca, the hate ran too deep. Dom stood and walked to Luca's desk. "Drink it," he said. Hate aside, there was still honor and professional courtesy.

Luca's hand shook, but he downed the scotch. Dom took the glass from him in his gloved hand and went to the bar to refill it, pouring generously. He returned to Luca's desk, setting the scotch in front of him. Without even making eye contact, Luca reached for the glass and drank.

Dom put the gun in Luca's hand, wrapping his gloved hand firmly around Luca's. He moved the gun to the side of Luca's head and pressed Luca's finger on the trigger.

Dom didn't bother to look. Luca wasn't worth his time. He'd told Angelina the same thing all those years ago. As he moved toward the door, he felt an uncharacteristic flash of optimism. The boss was a fair man, and loyalty was rewarded; the picture of the ring had been Luca's death sentence. *Maybe I can even find the actual ring.* It didn't need to stay in the wrong hands after all this time. He headed to the back of the house and engaged a blocking sequence that allowed him to exit while keeping the security system activated.

Chapter Forty-Two

Greg had just leaned back in his ergonomic office chair to review notes for an upcoming conference call when Nan knocked lightly and stepped in to place the day's mail in his inbox. He leaned forward and immediately spotted the large envelope from the private investigator he had hired to follow Chrystal. The PI had called him to let him know that he should expect some photos, telling Greg he had taken some interesting shots, and after Greg's review, he would be available if needed. *Perfect timing.*

Greg had spoken with Chrystal earlier in the week to let her know that he wouldn't be attending her last runway show. She had taken the news in an uncharacteristically nonchalant stride, which at first had puzzled him. But then his cynical side filled in the blanks. Most likely, she viewed being pregnant with his child as having secured for herself the needed degree of leverage. Now she could afford to be magnanimous with the little things. The money had been the goal all along. Greg wasn't hurt—he was pissed. How stupid of him! There had been plenty of signs about her true character that he had ignored. But at the end of the phone call, Greg had secured the only thing that mattered to him now—he had weaseled into joining her the following week for her doctor's appointment.

Greg slit the envelope carefully with his letter opener and removed several large black-and-white photographs and a letter. Greg scanned the document, which provided essentially the same information that the PI had shared over the telephone, along with the location for each site and the name of her companion. Greg shook his head when he read the name, Cash Endicott. He had really been negligent, or perhaps just not interested enough, to consider why she had not invited him to her runway shows over the last year. He wasn't sure why she had then invited him to this last one, but her reason, whatever it had been, wasn't relevant anymore.

The first picture had been taken in the same bar where Mindy had spotted Chrystal and Cash. They were sitting close together, and Chrystal's hand was resting on his thigh. They were both stylishly dressed. Cash was a handsome man and wore his dark hair long. Various shots from that same night and location showed Cash leaning in to tell her something, and Chrystal gazing into his eyes. Her expression stopped Greg cold. Her green eyes stared into Cash's face with an emotion he had never seen from her. It was the look of a woman who cared for the man she was with.

There was another set of photos from a coffee shop he recognized as close to Chrystal's condo. Both Cash and Chrystal had on athletic wear and baseball caps, and Greg couldn't help but think it looked like they had rolled out of bed and decided to get a coffee. Although the cap hid her hair, he didn't think she was even wearing makeup. Again, it was as if he were looking at a woman he had never met.

Greg stacked the photos together and gazed off into the distance, gathering his thoughts. He wasn't sure what he had expected to find when he'd decided to get a PI involved. At the most basic level, he supposed that he had been looking for leverage, perhaps even to use for getting sole custody. He had felt angry that he had put himself into a position where a woman whom he did not respect or like would have the right to raise his child. And he had felt sad about how his actions could affect Rheagan. What he hadn't expected was that looking at these pictures might make him question whether he was even the child's father. Whatever was going on between Chrystal and Cash did not look new or shallow. The two of them had been or still were significantly connected.

Greg turned to his computer and brought up the search engine. He had some more investigating to do.

Chapter Forty-Three

On Sunday morning, the sunlight shining into Greg's bedroom window actually woke him. *That isn't the norm,* he mused sleepily. Getting up, he made himself a pot of coffee and took his first cup of the strong black brew out to the deck overlooking the water. He was looking forward to seeing Rheagan today. Their relationship, though still on somewhat of a hold based on his situation with Chrystal, felt rich and satisfying in ways he had never imagined for himself. The week had been a busy one for both of them—late restaurant hours for her, and his prepping for a trial in Boise on a contested will. However, today, they were meeting at 11:00 in his office to review Mike's computer. Then they planned to catch some lunch and play it by ear. He felt his pulse quicken just thinking of holding her in his arms again.

At 11:00 a.m. sharp, he heard Rheagan open the front door of his office suite, and he left his own office to meet her in the entryway, pulling her in for a long, slow, delicious kiss. "I think Sunday is my new favorite day … given that it's the only day we both have off," he said, reaching for her hand and leading her

toward his office. "Let's get this over with so we can enjoy the rest of the day."

Rheagan squeezed his hand in response as she followed. "As I told you earlier, I never even thought to look at his history. What made you think of it?"

Greg's expression turned serious, and he paused before speaking. "Well, it's the one place we haven't checked yet. Given what we have discovered about the safe-deposit box and his phones, it occurred to me that Mike had carefully planned it all. But since his death was an accident, he might have still had something saved on the laptop that he hadn't cleaned up yet."

He saw Rheagan blanch, and he squeezed her shoulder. "Honey, I'm sorry to stress you with this, it's just that I didn't want to do it without your knowledge. Maybe we should ask the sheriff to do it for us. But I'm not sure he's taking us seriously, and more than anything, I want to know you're safe."

He saw her swallow hard, but then she nodded. "It's okay, I get it. Let's do it."

Greg had already plugged Mike's laptop in, and while Rheagan seated herself, he hit the power button. The computer came to life. When the prompt for a password came up, they looked at each other. "I don't suppose you know it?" he asked her.

Rheagan shook her head. "I think we're going to have to guess for a while."

"We may need those professionals after all. We might have only so many chances before the operating system locks up for security purposes." Greg sighed. "Imagine Sheriff Jansen's face if we go in asking for assistance on checking for hidden files and search history on Mike's computer, having frozen it up with password attempts."

Despite herself, Rheagan laughed. They tried birthdays, names, addresses, and combinations of each. Greg was about to give up in frustration when Rheagan suggested the Minnesota Twins or some variation of that. Greg nodded his head in affirmation and then began typing. The first two attempts came up empty, but then he typed in "twincitiestwins," and the computer began the start-up sequence.

Greg turned and looked at Rheagan; her face was ashen again, but she nodded. He went to *File Explorer* and then to *View,* where he checked a box to make hidden files visible. Rheagan looked over his shoulder to see if she could spot any files or folders that she hadn't noticed before.

"Oh my God," she said. "There's a folder called *Twins.*"

Greg clicked on the folder to open it, and a single file named "resume" was inside. He clicked on the file, and Mike's resume filled the screen. The most recent job listed was that of chef/co-owner at Savor.

Greg heard Rheagan gasp behind him, and he reached out to bring her close. Tears were streaming down her face. "He was planning to leave …"

Greg held her until her crying stopped, and the outpouring of emotion had drained the still, pale and fragile woman who now sat beside him. "Do you want to get out of here?" he asked with concern.

She shook her head. "Let's make sure there's nothing else here." And with that, she leaned forward and directed her gaze to the screen.

They found no additional files, but recent web history showed he had been browsing restaurant scenes in several large cities: Chicago, Houston, and even New York City. Greg reached for her hand and said, "I would like to bring you home with me. What do you say?"

"I would like that," Rheagan said, still quiet and distant, but the color was coming back to her face. He held her hand as they walked out into the sunshine and didn't let go until they reached his Land Rover.

"I'm sorry, Rheagan." Greg reached over the console, lifting her chin so that her eyes met his. "I didn't want to hurt you further. I'm surprised by this, too," he said soberly, and she nodded.

Chapter Forty-Four

Greg started his vehicle, and they drove the short distance to his home. When he opened his front door and ushered her inside, Rheagan felt the calming effect that his home always had on her. Still holding her hand, he led her to the kitchen, which, for obvious reasons as a chef, was her favorite room of all.

"Let's see … I'm going to make us some cheese, crackers, and fruit. I think this day calls for some wine, but I also have coffee, and sparkling water?"

Rheagan gave him a trembling smile. "Definitely the wine."

Rheagan sat at the counter for a moment, absorbing the day's events while Greg moved around the kitchen. Somehow, Greg knew she was still feeling overwhelmed because he materialized beside her and just drew her into his arms.

"Honey, we've got this." He handed her a glass of wine and set a platter in front of her. Grabbing his own wine glass and some napkins, he took the seat beside her.

She nodded her head and gave him a watery smile. "Greg, thank you. I'm so lucky to have had your support through all of this. Do you think that discussing what our relationships with Mike were like, especially at the end, might help us better understand all of this? If we're going to be in a relationship of our own, I don't want there to be secrets between us, especially relating to Mike."

Greg nodded, and Rheagan took a long breath. "When Mike and I met in culinary school, we had both been there for almost a year, so we both knew a lot of other students. Once we began falling in love, it seemed natural to become each other's world, so maybe because of that, I didn't realize how little time he spent with others. It wasn't until we moved to Whisper Island that I began to understand that Mike really only cared about being with you and me. He would tolerate others, but it was clear to me that he wasn't really present or interested in forming friendships with anyone else, including my parents and even our staff." She sighed deeply. "It took a toll on me. I tried to talk to him, but those discussions didn't move the needle."

Greg nodded again, encouraging her to go on.

"A month or so before his accident, he told me that he wasn't sure he wanted to have children. He said he felt the two of us were good together and didn't want us to change. He asked me to think about it for a while, and we could discuss it further when I was ready. Greg, I'm not sure I was even surprised." Her voice faltered. "I had begun to wonder if I was living the life that I would have chosen for myself. He was such a strong and driving presence that I felt I was letting him push me along. Almost as if in satisfying his needs, there wouldn't be enough room left for me." Rheagan was sobbing now, her shoulders shaking.

Greg picked up a napkin from the counter and handed it to Rheagan, pulling her close into his shoulder. He held her there tightly, wrapping his arms around her, while the storm of emotions passed through her body. As the tears began to slow, she pushed herself upright and looked into his eyes. "And then he was gone, and we never finished that discussion, and then … and then …" the sobs started again. "And then I received all that money for Savor, and then the life insurance …"

Greg tipped her tear-streaked face up so that her eyes met his. "And you've been taking on guilt for all of this?" She nodded, still crying, but continuing to meet his eyes. Greg brought her in for another long, healing hug. And then he spoke, "Rheagan, I hear what you're saying, and I can relate. I had many similar situations with Mike here and in college—a reluctance on his part to join in and include others in our friendship. I did my own share of buffering between him and Sam, just as one example. I am sure that being his partner was an even more intense experience. He had obviously been to Whisper Island since he visited here on school breaks, but I must admit that I was surprised when he decided to move here. For the very reasons you mentioned. As you said, Mike was high-energy and restless. I did warn him about the close-knit community when he told me he wanted to come, but his mind was made up. Building Savor with you must have held his focus for a while."

Rheagan felt the tightness in her chest begin to lessen with Greg's words. *He's validating what I felt.* "Do you think he would have left without telling us? And would he have been leaving because he thought he had to for our safety, or was he just ready to move on? Apparently, having children together felt like too much commitment …" She dabbed tears with the back of her sleeve. "I know it was hard for him to feel tied down. I'd always thought of him as a free spirit, but I hadn't accepted he would never settle down."

"My guess is he was exploring his options. I remain convinced that he felt a strong and lasting bond with us, so

I can't believe he would have moved on without a word. His relationship with the two of us was too strong for me to believe that he would have just ghosted us. I have to think he thought that deleting his photos and contacts and locking up the photos in the safe-deposit box was enough to ensure our safety, and my guess is that he was torn on whether to stay or go."

Greg reached for her hand and held it gently. "Over the years, Mike and I had numerous conversations about women—he generally viewed them as manipulative and selfish. But you were different, and he knew it—he asked you to marry him, after all." Greg ran his other hand through his hair and sighed. He let his hand drop to the table, and his body seemed to still, as if he was lost in his thoughts. Finally, he spoke. "Rheagan, I sat across from him while we crafted those legal agreements. Regardless of whether he was prepared to settle down here long term, I feel certain that Mike would have wanted you to thrive and to keep Savor."

Rheagan felt her eyes begin streaming again.

"Mike loved us both—I remain sure of that," Greg said. "But you had every right to question whether the future he was offering was what you wanted."

Rheagan nodded, feeling lighter because of their discussion. She had shared her last secret, and Greg had responded with his typical non-judgmental logic. *I am so lucky to have him in my life.*

Greg raised his wine glass and pointed at her full one, "If you don't drink that, I will think you are a wine snob."

Rheagan smiled back at him and took a big sip.

Because lunch had been just cheese and fruit, Rheagan offered to check out his pantry and see what she could find to work with for dinner. "How do you feel about a lazy version of spaghetti carbonara?" she asked.

"How can you pull that off with what's in this house?" Greg asked, looking incredulous.

"A little chef magic," Rheagan said, taking eggs, bacon, and a block of Parmesan cheese from his refrigerator. She opened his freezer and found a bag of frozen green peas. "It may not be fancy, but it will be good." She brushed past him to get the pasta from his pantry, and he pulled her in for a long and very sexy kiss.

They were both breathing hard when he finally pulled back, looking into her eyes, and said, "In an effort to be sensitive to everything you've been through today, I delayed doing that as long as I possibly could …"

"Mmm, that kiss tells me that despite all of this, we have a lot to look forward to."

Greg pulled her in again for a big hug. "We definitely do."

Rheagan enjoyed preparing the meal in Greg's fabulous kitchen. There was so much space to prep, and the appliances were so much nicer than what she had in her apartment. Greg kept her wine glass filled, and he kept pulling her in for more long, slow kisses. *He is driving me crazy with those sexy lips …* With a startled yelp, she grabbed the pasta water before it boiled over, and they shared a laugh.

Greg set the table with plates, napkins, and cutlery, and Rheagan dished up their plates. Topping off their wine glasses and sitting down beside her, he took his first bite. "So delicious! Ms. Rossi, you've been a hell of a distraction, but now I realize how little I've had to eat today."

"Are you sure about violating the slow track?" Greg asked while kissing her lips as he walked her backward toward his bed.

"Absolutely." She felt the mattress behind her knees and the feeling of weightlessness as he gently pushed her down. Still kissing her lips, he managed to land beside her on the luxurious king bed. Propping himself up on one arm, he gently pushed her long hair away from her face and looked down into her eyes. His expression was serious, almost fierce, and one hundred percent sexy male. Rheagan reached her own arms up and pulled his face down to hers, capturing his lips. With a groan, his hands began moving greedily over her body, and she felt the flare of that delectable electricity consume her. The sex was both silly and serious, and they took their time, luxuriating in the feel and taste of each other. Along with the intoxicating heat of their attraction, Rheagan felt the fulfilling bond of their emotional connection.

Chapter Forty-Five

Greg had an out-of-town business trip scheduled for a few days. The timing of the meeting frustrated him because he was focused on Chrystal's pregnancy, but he asked Nan to reschedule some local meetings on his calendar so he could see Chrystal again. *I'm glad I made time to meet at her condo before we go to her doctor's appointment.* When he reached her building, she buzzed him in and met him at her door. Leading him to the living room, she offered him a coffee or water, which he declined. Instead, he decided to open the discussion directly. The pictures, even if he didn't fully understand them, made him even more determined not to entertain any more of her games. "Chrystal, I have become aware that you are in a relationship with Cash."

She had been pouring herself a sparkling water when he began speaking, and now she turned to him. She stood very still, almost as if she were considering her next move. Maybe she was. She must have reasoned that she couldn't deny it entirely because she set the glass down. "We do have a past. We've known each other for years, and both of us know that we aren't good together. Anyway, now that I'm pregnant with our child, I don't understand what Cash has to do with anything." Greg saw only confidence in her green eyes.

"Chrystal, I don't see a future for us, and I'm not sure I trust you in this situation. If you are pregnant, and if it is my child, we will need to reach an agreement. In the short term, I would like a DNA test to verify that I am indeed the father of your baby. There is a non-invasive paternity test that can be performed at this stage in your pregnancy."

She didn't show any outward physical reaction to his words, but the look in her eyes seemed to shift from confidence to calculation. He shook his head slowly and stood. "Chrystal, you might be interested in these." He laid the pictures down on the bar counter beside her. She glanced at the top one, the picture of her hand on Cash's thigh, and her expression went flat.

Chapter Forty-Six

Rheagan showed an older couple who had just dropped in to try an herb-infused drink to a table for two. For the first time all evening, she had a moment to herself. *I miss Greg … Getting off work isn't the same without seeing him.* He had traveled to Boise for a couple of days to attend to some depositions in his contested will case. They were calling and texting every day, but she still missed just being in his company … and in his bed. He had promised to call her from his hotel later, and he would be catching a plane home in the morning.

The night had been a busy one. Savor had been completely booked, and several tables from the last reservation were still occupied, showing no signs of leaving. Another round of drinks was being served. Tonight had been another cross-promotion event with Charlie's bottle shop, and the tequila cilantro lemonades were a huge hit. She imagined Mike's reaction to cilantro being in his kitchen and felt a smile curve her lips. From her vantage point near the front, she viewed the lingering diners. Honestly, she was just as pleased that it was going to be a late night and delighted to see that the new menu items were popular.

Eventually, the restaurant began to empty, and Rheagan and the team started their closing duties. She reached for her phone in her pocket, but it was empty. She groaned. *I must have left it in the apartment earlier.*

She straightened the already-neat items on the hostess stand, then detoured to the kitchen to say a quick goodnight to Joe, and headed up the back stairs to her apartment. As she approached her front door, she stopped for a minute. *Do I smell smoke? Like cigar smoke?* She shook her head and reached for the door handle; it felt loose, but when she inserted her key, the door opened easily. Later, she would be amazed at how careless she had been not to realize the signs of a forced entry, but it wasn't until she rounded the corner and saw the sofa cushions ripped open and her things tossed into the center of the room that she realized what she had walked into. Her adrenaline kicked in, and she knew she should turn around and leave, yet she stood frozen. *Please, God, let Mr. Pickles be okay.* A furry feline missile launched himself into her arms, and she caught his body awkwardly. Then she turned and ran back down the hall toward the stairs and Savor.

She burst into the restaurant, calling for Joe, and he hurried in from the kitchen, stopping short when he saw her strained face and Mr. Pickles in her arms. "What the hell! Are you okay?"

"Someone broke into my apartment!"

"Okay, let me call 911, and you need to sit down," he said, grabbing her by the arm and leading her to a chair. Rheagan sat down heavily, still holding Mr. Pickles, who was making no effort to leave the security of her arms.

Joe grabbed his phone and punched in the numbers, not taking his eyes off of hers. Almost immediately after he ended the call, they heard sirens approaching, and he left her, returning quickly with a glass of water.

"Thank you, Joe. I'm so thankful you were still here …"

"Me too," he said, going to open the front door for the arriving officers. Rheagan recognized both Officers Nelson and Officer Robbins. Whisper Island was a small community, and almost everyone was acquainted at least on a casual basis.

They walked in quickly. "Ms. Rossi, we understand there was a break-in at your residence on the upper floor. We're going to secure the area, and we'll be back to take your statement."

Joe led them over to the back stairs entrance, using his fob to let them into the staircase and then returned to Rheagan's side.

"Joe, it's late, so you can go on home if you're done here. I'm okay now that the police are here," Rheagan offered with a tired smile.

"Forget about it—I'm staying until I know you are safe. And I don't think you should stay here tonight."

Rheagan nodded. "I think I will ask them to let me get some things and drop me off at the resort." She didn't tell Joe about the ripped-apart sofa cushions and her suspicion that her mattress had endured a similar fate. Someone had been looking for something, and she felt deeply grateful for Greg's foresight in removing all evidence of the photos and searches into Mike's past.

Joe signaled his approval. They heard the beep of the rear door opening to the outside, and in minutes, both officers rejoined them inside Savor. "The premises have been secured, but we'd like to get some information from you, Rheagan."

"Absolutely," she responded, and then turned to Joe. "Please go on home now. And Joe, thanks again."

"Of course. Call if you need me," Joe said, squeezing her shoulder as he turned to leave.

Still holding Mr. Pickles, Rheagan followed Officers Nelson and Robbins back upstairs to her apartment. "I was distracted, and it was already a late night." Her voice sounded shrill to her own ears, and she was talking fast. She took a breath and resumed speaking. "I noticed cigar smoke, and I'm embarrassed to admit, I rationalized it away—it just seemed too crazy. The door lock felt loose, but when I rattled it, it was locked. I was entering the living room when I saw the mess, and I panicked for a moment about my cat. But then he jumped into my arms, so I ran back down to Savor, and Joe called you."

"Ms. Rossi, it appears that your outside exit door has been damaged, and that is likely the point of entry. And, ma'am, the apartment lock should be upgraded—it's a relatively easy lock to pick."

Rheagan nodded and paused for a moment. "Greg Andersen and I spoke to Sheriff Jansen recently about some issues regarding Mike, my late fiancé. The two of you may want to touch base with the sheriff, as that discussion may relate to this break-in."

The two officers exchanged a significant look, but Rheagan was too tired and stressed to interpret it.

They walked with her through her apartment and her offices as she attempted to identify the items that had been taken. Her laptop and cell phone were clearly missing. When she explained that she had been using a burner recently, the two officers exchanged another meaningful look, but Rheagan didn't elaborate—Sheriff Jansen could fill them in. It was clear to all three of them that the break-in had been a search for something.

Officer Nelson suggested that she pack some things and spend the night elsewhere. In total agreement, she put Mr.

Pickles in his carrier and searched through the mess for what they would need. Taking one more look at her devastated apartment, she felt the tears well up. She had been right about her mattress—it had been cut open. And again, like the living room, her items littered the floor. Things were no better in her closets and offices, or the powder room and primary bath—everything was a mess. Whoever had been there had left no stone unturned, and the stale smell of cigars and something sweeter still permeated the air.

As she returned to her living room with Mr. Pickles' carrier and her overnight necessities, she noticed the two officers exchanging yet another significant glance. Officer Nelson spoke, "We just updated Sheriff Jansen on your situation, and he has instructed us to post an officer near your room at the resort tonight. He also asked us to inform you that he will be reaching out to WITSEC, the witness protection agency, in the morning. Ms. Rossi, we will likely need to be in your apartment and possibly the restaurant over the next couple of days, so you might need to make some arrangements in the morning."

Rheagan nodded. She felt the suffocating weight of sadness for what seemed like damning confirmation that the man she had loved had dealt with too much throughout his too-short life. She felt immensely grateful that she had never shared her doubts about their shared future with him. *He'd clearly already lived through enough hard stuff.* She followed the two officers to their patrol car.

Chapter Forty-Seven

Greg awoke from a fitful doze around midnight in Boise to the ringing of his hotel phone. Gripping the receiver, he heard Rheagan's voice, sounding weak and trembling on the other end. "Rheagan! Where have you been? I've been texting and calling." He sat bolt upright in his hotel bed when he heard what sounded like a sniffle.

"Greg … my apartment was robbed. They … they … cut all my cushions and trashed the place …" She was sobbing now.

Hearing the sadness and the fear in her voice made him feel broken. He should have been there for her, but instead, she'd had to face this all by herself. "Rheagan, honey, are you okay? Where are you?"

He heard her draw a deep breath, and then she said in a trembling tone, "I'm okay. I'm in a room at the resort."

"Tell me what happened, honey," Greg said, trying to understand the situation better.

"I tried to text you as I was leaving Savor, and that's when I realized I had left my phone upstairs. When I got to my apartment, I saw the mess and froze. Mr. Pickles jumped at me, and I just grabbed him and ran back down to Savor. Joe was there and called the cops. And Greg … Sheriff Jansen has an officer posted by my door."

"Good for him, I'm glad that he's taking your welfare seriously. Honey, I'm so sorry that I'm not there with you."

"I wish you were here too," she said. "Hurry home, okay?"

"Deal. Are you going to be able to get some sleep?"

"I think so. I feel safe. I got to talk to you, and I have Mr. Pickles with me."

"Okay, honey, get some rest, and I will be on the first plane home to you. And Rheagan, I love you." Greg realized what he'd just said. *It's true, and I can't help but tell her.* His chest filled with emotion as he heard a pause.

"Oh, Greg, I love you too." Rheagan's voice sounded stronger and yet soft. Greg thought it sounded like she was smiling.

"Can you fall asleep now?" Greg asked quietly after another meaningful pause.

"Yes, I'm sure I can," Rheagan assured him. "I'll be fine. I'm snuggling with Mr. Pickles, and hearing your voice, especially what you just told me, makes me feel warm and secure."

Chapter Forty-Eight

Agent Jim Barrett boarded the flight from WITSEC headquarters to Seattle, Washington. He would take a seaplane from there to Whisper Island. He knew the route—it wasn't his first trip there. He carried with him a laptop and a small briefcase, but most of what he needed for this meeting was in his head. He had spent his entire career at WITSEC, and he had so many stories that would never be told, many of which would not have been believed had he been allowed to speak. But this story, the one involving Mike, always pulled at his heartstrings because he had been there from the beginning.

WITSEC cases sometimes went dormant, as this one had. Using proper protocols, it was determined that the risk-to-benefit ratio did not warrant active status. Still, as a precautionary measure, routine low-level surveillance was generally deemed advisable.

Because of this surveillance, the suicide of a rising senator from Philadelphia had been communicated to him at WITSEC. On the surface, the evidence did indeed support a suicide. Senator Bianchi had been alone in his home. The home was equipped with a fully operational security system that was activated at the time of death. Senator Bianchi's fingerprints were on the gun, and while there was no suicide note, threatening letters incriminating him for favors obtained through mob ties were found on his desk. Senator Bianchi had recently thrown his hat into the ring for a gubernatorial post. It was widely believed that the increased attention had led to his being blackmailed.

Agent Barrett had been aware of Senator Bianchi for many years, going back to when he was just handsome Luca Bianchi, who believed he deserved better than following in the South Philly "family" business. In his opinion, Luca was far too arrogant to think anyone could stop his ascension, so suicide was not a given.

The next domino to fall had been the suicide of Angelina Bonasera. Even though she had an apartment in Los Angeles, she had killed herself by jumping out of a disreputable establishment's window in a different part of the city. Angelina had been in WITSEC for eighteen years, using the assumed names Angie D'oro and, later, Anna Carlucci, before opting out of the program and returning to her original identity.

Agent Barrett had been delighted to see her go. When Angelina departed, she had severed all ties to her eighteen-year-old son, Michael Carlucci, who remained in the program and had the opportunity to attend college and build a life apart from the constant, malignant chaos of his mother. According to agency protocols, Agent Barrett had remained in periodic contact with Mike, who had thrived in the years following his mother's departure.

In a perfect world, Agent Barrett would never have heard of Angelina again, but unfortunately, she'd returned to his radar screen ten months ago when Mike informed him that she had sent him an email. Despite her promises and her knowledge of the danger to Mike, she had googled his name and reached out to congratulate him on his restaurant. Mike had been understandably alarmed. He knew first-hand how reckless and self-serving his mother could be. By using her original identity, Angelina might have inadvertently alerted the mob to the existence of a love child between Luca and her, and established a direct tie for them to reach him.

Agent Barrett and Mike had both agreed that after all these years, the likelihood of any interest by the mob was low. Still, the agent had added Angelina Bonasera's name to the low-level surveillance list due to her troublesome behavior. And that was how he'd been notified of a suicide victim without ID who at first appeared to be homeless but was later identified as Angelina Bonasera. Angelina's death had actually occurred before Luca's, but the delay in identifying her body had reversed the order in which Agent Barrett was notified.

And now, in another supposedly random act, the home of Mike's fiancée, Rheagan Rossi, had been broken into and searched. Sheriff Jansen of Whisper Island had contacted WITSEC, forwarding the files from his meetings with Rheagan and Greg, as well as the recent break-in, and Agent Barrett had elected to make the trip personally. He needed to see the evidence himself and speak to the most important people in Mike's life.

While it was easy for the agent to conclude that the three on-the-surface "unrelated" events were most certainly "related," he was still questioning the "why." After all these years, why had these three individuals, as a unit, become of interest to the mob again? Still, based on facts garnered through regular intelligence channels and some well-placed informants, he felt comfortable with his working theory. So, now Agent Barrett wanted to talk to Ms. Rossi and Mr. Andersen. He wanted to see whether their stories corroborated his theory so that he could close this chapter.

Agent Barrett knew better than anyone how Mike had been affected by the WITSEC process and by being raised by a selfish, troubled teenager. WITSEC wasn't designed to facilitate family situations like the one Mike had fallen into. Things could have been different for Mike if Angelina hadn't gotten them pulled from Minneapolis. Her decision to use the local mafia as her dating pool had risked not only her life but Mike's, too.

He recalled that, when he was an adult on his own, Mike had told him more than once that he felt different from others. He said he didn't feel he could care about people the way they expected him to. But Agent Barrett knew that somehow, Greg and Rheagan had come closer than anyone else. He also knew that Mike had still been undecided about staying on Whisper Island—the small island had begun to feel like pressure to him because of the tight social network there. Mike had also been questioning whether he could give Rheagan what he felt she deserved. Mike's recent struggles had made Agent Barrett concerned for Mike. He'd hoped the younger man would stay and work through his fears. But then Anna had reached out, endangering not just him, but the only two people he had allowed himself to love. And then, ultimately, fate had cut Mike's future short.

Agent Barrett sighed as he rubbed his face with his hand. He intended to meet Greg and Rheagan first and then determine how much of Mike's story to share with them.

He closed his eyes and let his mind wander. *Ahh, Mike … playing with fire, keeping those pictures of Angelina. But it's almost harder knowing you kept the baseball stub from the game I took you to see in Minneapolis. You didn't have nearly as many good things in your life as you deserved.*

Chapter Forty-Nine

As soon as he landed on Whisper Island, Greg dialed Rheagan at the hotel. "Hey, I'm back and want to see you. Where are you?"

She sucked in a deep breath. "Oh, Greg, I'm so glad you're here. I'm just leaving the resort and heading back home to meet Officer Nelson. He's going to let me into my apartment so I can pick up a few additional things."

"Can I meet you there?"

"I would love that." Rheagan felt her unshed tears rise. Greg was back, and she would have his strength to lean on. She had spent a restless morning in her room at the resort, half-watching the morning news and holding Mr. Pickles. She was so thankful that he had not been hurt during the vandalism of her apartment.

She had called Joe first thing that morning to tell him that Savor needed to be closed for a few days. He had offered to let the rest of the team know, and Rheagan had thankfully agreed.

He had been concerned for her and likely curious, but she really couldn't tell him much more than the obvious. Her home had been broken into, and it was a crime scene. She still hadn't shared that the apartment had been ransacked and searched. At this point, she felt she needed the sheriff's permission to impart any details, even with her employees. However, Whisper Island was a small community, and she knew it wouldn't take long for word to get out that an officer was guarding her hotel room.

Rheagan pulled her RAV4 up to Savor and saw that both Greg and Officer Nelson were waiting for her. Greg came over to her car as she was closing the door and enveloped her in a long hug. In the warmth and security of his embrace, she stemmed the tears that threatened to spill over and just let herself feel like part of a team. She had faced so many hard things since Mike's death, and Greg had always been there and now even more so. She brushed the tears from her eyes, and with Greg holding her hand, they walked toward Officer Nelson.

The three of them looked at the back entrance, where the crime scene tape flagged the door. Officer Nelson pointed out the scratches and evidence that a tool had been used to pry the door open. "Why didn't my security system alarm go off?" Rheagan asked the officer.

"Ms. Rossi, I apologize, but the sheriff has asked me to have you hold your questions for now. He would like you to head to his office once you have gathered what you need from your apartment."

"Okay." Rheagan nodded. "Greg, will you come with me?"

"Of course," he replied reassuringly, following her up the stairs with Officer Nelson at the rear.

When she opened the door, she braced herself for what she would find. In the light of day, the destruction and violation of her home felt even more devastating. Without the shock element, she could focus on the brutal knife cuts to her cushions and the deliberate and reckless damage to the possessions of a lifetime. She heard Greg's muffled exclamation and felt his arms come around her.

Officer Nelson appeared in the doorway. "Again, Ms. Rossi, as much as possible, if you could try not to disturb anything since this is still a crime scene."

She nodded silently and headed toward her bedroom to see what she could find in her ransacked closet.

Sheriff Jansen stood when he saw Rheagan and Greg at his door and waved for them to take the seats across from his desk. Folding his hands, he leaned forward, he focused on Rheagan. "Ms. Rossi, I am sorry for the business at your apartment last night, and I hope that you are feeling better today."

"Thank you, Sheriff. I'm okay."

"Based on the nature of the break-in at your apartment and on the information you both shared with me earlier this week, I placed a call to WITSEC this morning. It appears that your suspicions about what you have discovered since Mike's death are indeed related in some manner to the witness protection program."

Rheagan felt the crushing sadness of Mike's history again. Greg reached over and took her hand, holding it as the sheriff paused to let his words sink in.

Sheriff Jansen continued. "I was put in touch with Agent Barrett, who handled Mike's case. Agent Barrett is here now on Whisper Island, and his office will be taking over this investigation. My office is providing him with working space, and my officers will continue to provide security detail for you under Agent Barrett's direction." He paused again to see if they had questions. Then he said, "Agent Barrett is going to want to process your apartment for evidence, so he is asking that you not enter your apartment or restaurant without a police escort until further notice. He's asked that you meet him here at 4:00 p.m. today."

Rheagan nodded, her mind overwhelmed by the situation. Squeezing her hand, Greg spoke, "Sheriff, may Rheagan relocate from the resort to my home?"

Sheriff Jansen's focus panned from Rheagan to Greg. "That is a question for Agent Barrett. He may prefer that we keep Rheagan at the resort at night, as it is a more confined space for security purposes."

Greg nodded. "Of course, Sheriff. Just to let you know, I will be talking with Ms. Rossi about perhaps joining her there tonight."

Sheriff Jansen nodded his head in acknowledgement. "One last thing, Ms. Rossi. If the two of you have any further concerns, outside the scope covered by Agent Barrett, please give my office a call."

Chapter Fifty

Agent Barrett pushed back his chair and stood to greet Rheagan and Greg when they entered his borrowed office in the sheriff's department building later that afternoon. He was a tall, lean man with salt-and-pepper hair and a serious yet pleasant face. "Ms. Rossi and Mr. Andersen, my name is Agent Barrett. Thank you for joining me."

Greg handed the box he was carrying to Agent Barrett, who set it on the edge of the desk. Then they shook the agent's hand before taking their seats in the two chairs across from his desk.

The agent leaned toward them, clasping his hands, and gave them a smile tinged with sadness. "First of all, I want to say how sorry I am about Mike's death. That loss was no doubt hard enough, and now you've had to deal with this business. I think it's pretty apparent to the two of you that the WITSEC program is not in the business of divulging details about participants in the program, nor the reasons why they became involved in the program. However, we can sometimes share selected facts or observations. I hope to review the items you found in the safe-deposit box, hear your thoughts, and, to some degree, help you come to terms with all this."

Greg was holding Rheagan's hand, and she felt the reassuring squeeze of his fingers as they both nodded at Agent Barrett.

"First of all, I would like to start with the incident that took Mike's life. I want to assure you both that WITSEC performed our own independent investigation into that occurrence shortly after Mike's death, and we are in agreement with the sheriff's office that it was indeed a tragic accident."

Rheagan felt the rush of tears and felt the squeeze of Greg's fingers again.

Agent Barrett directed his gaze to her, and she saw his own sorrow reflected on his serious face. "Ms. Rossi, could you please share with me the items you found in the safe-deposit box on Seal Island?"

Rheagan nodded, and Greg stood to help her retrieve the items from the box. "I found his old cell phone." She held it out. "A couple of months before he died, he told me he'd lost his phone, but there it was in the safe-deposit box." Rheagan sighed. "I also found an envelope containing two pictures and a baseball ticket stub. The bank manager included this log of activity for the account."

Agent Barrett opened the envelope first, extracting the pictures and ticket stub, then nodded and laid them down. They were just as they'd appeared in the file of evidence from the sheriff. He glanced briefly at the log and set it down beside the pictures. "I understand you were able to access this phone, but that it was missing numerous photos?"

"Yes," Greg responded. "The folks at Apple informed me that Mike had taken steps to delete specific data from the phone permanently. From what we can see, the data deleted was all of the photos and information related to either Rheagan or me."

Agent Barrett nodded and then asked, "So, tell me about removing the electronics from Ms. Rossi's home and office. I understand that your action was precipitated by a trip to SeaTac and a trip to Philadelphia."

"Yes, switching out her devices was my idea," Greg said. "It was after Rheagan received the handwritten warning at the restaurant in Philly, telling her to go home and leave things alone—that note is in this box as well. Anyway, I became uneasy and wanted to remove any evidence of her having seen those old photos of Mike's and her online searches of them from her home and business."

Agent Barrett smiled wryly and tapped Mike's cell phone, which was still lying on the desk. "There seems to be a rash of that going on at Whisper Island of late."

Rheagan couldn't stop the quick, nervous laugh from the unexpected humor, and she could see that Greg was smiling too.

"Well, Mr. Andersen, I commend you on your quick and preventative actions regarding the electronics, and by your actions to involve your local sheriff's office in your concerns as well." The agent smiled again at the two of them and then sat back in a contemplative mode.

Finally, he broke his silence. "In my experience, there are few, if any, coincidences in the cases we see at WITSEC. In general, we view these cases through the lens of cause and effect." He paused and smiled wryly. "In my opinion, this situation presents an interesting blend of coincidence and cause-and-effect."

"Let me begin with what I see as the cause-and-effect portion. The situation that brought Mike into the WITSEC program occurred before his birth." Agent Barrett shook his head slightly. "The inciting event was entirely internal to the mob and would normally have never even reached our radar. It involved a messy love triangle and a father who had been warned and had failed to control his daughter. Mike's birth mother, whom you know by her WITSEC name as Anna, was the center of the trouble. It was Anna herself who approached WITSEC, but ultimately, it was deemed that she was neither credible nor did she have sufficient evidence to testify. The agents working the case, including myself, became quickly disillusioned by Anna's bait-and-switch tactics, but it was decided that she would be at risk if released."

The agent paused to make sure they were following, and when both Rheagan and Greg nodded, he spoke again. "Given the lack of a trial and the span of years since the inciting event, the situation appeared dormant. However, we believe that recently someone connected to the situation shared knowledge of Anna's here-to-unknown pregnancy and voiced concerns that if discovered, it could create a reputational risk. That risk could in turn derail a mob-related opportunity. We believe that the sharing of Anna's pregnancy triggered a chain of events, including the ransacking of your apartment, Ms. Rossi. We believe that your apartment was searched solely for evidence relating to Anna, her past, and any identification of Michael's birth father that might connect him to the inciting event."

Agent Barrett paused again, taking a sip from the water bottle on his desk. "It is our opinion that the next part of this story was a completely separate track and only by coincidence of the timing seemed to be related. We believe that your discovery of Mike's safe deposit box, your visit to his high school and neighborhood, and even your trip to Philadelphia and the restaurant were in no way connected to the break-in at your apartment. While Franco's restaurant has been known to be frequented by the mob, he is not connected to the mob. He would, however, have recognized both Anna and the young man in the photo. We believe he was trying to warn you off out of kindness."

Agent Barrett rested his elbows on the desk and leaned forward. "We also believe that Greg's foresight in removing all the electronics and safe-deposit contents from your home and business, and the timing of that removal, was key. In our opinion, the mob's interest in Mike's situation has come to an end. They were looking for evidence of Mike's past connections, and you've left nothing on site for them to discover. Likewise, nothing will be found from their search of your electronics.

"I realize that you probably have a lot of questions I haven't answered. We generally believe that in these situations, it is best to be discreet. Still, I'd love to hear your thoughts." Agent Barrett sat back in his chair and took another drink from his bottle of water.

Greg spoke. "Can you elaborate any further on why we should feel confident that the mob's interest in this situation has ended?"

"Good question, Greg, and a valid one." Agent Barrett nodded. "I won't go into the details, since the chain of events that I mentioned earlier involved several situations that I am not at liberty to talk about. However, I can tell you that what these situations share is that, while we believe they were all mob-related, in each instance, the mob went out of its way to hide its involvement. That is the case with your break-in, too, Ms. Rossi. In a typical investigation into what occurred at your home, the police would have concluded that it was likely a quick drug-motivated toss focused on high-ticket saleable items, cash, etc. In our experience, when the mob hides their prints from situations related to WITSEC, it means they don't want to bring any further attention to the original inciting event."

"Can you share any details about why Mike's cell phone was in the safe-deposit box and why he deleted his history?" Rheagan asked.

Agent Barrett paused for an extended moment before answering. "Mike became concerned by press related to the opening of your shared restaurant. There had been a couple of articles on Savor. Out of an abundance of caution, he wanted to minimize attention on either you or Greg. Mike and I discussed it, and he felt it was the decision he was comfortable with."

The agent paused again. "I want to share with you both how much the two of you meant to him in his life. Most people don't realize the day-to-day struggles of a participant in the WITSEC program. It is difficult for them to form attachments to others because of the burden of their own secrets. Mike struggled with that as much as anyone." Agent Barrett smiled sadly. "I had the privilege of watching Mike grow up, and I think I know him as well as anyone because with me, he could talk freely. I can tell you this. You may have sensed areas where he struggled—he would want you to know it wasn't because of you."

Rheagan realized she was crying, and Agent Barrett passed her a tissue from a Kleenex box on his desk.

"I'm guessing you were the uncle whom his neighbor mentioned he went to live with after high school?" she heard Greg ask.

Agent Barrett nodded. "I did remove him from SeaTac and set him up at UW, but the 'uncle' story came from Mike.

WITSEC does not provide any narrative around our actions, but it is very common for participants like Mike to want to provide friends with a degree of closure."

Greg sighed and then said, "After we spoke to the sheriff, against his advice, we performed one more search on Mike's laptop—which you will see when you process it. We discovered a secret file containing Mike's resume. It was recent enough to include his ownership of Savor. We also found web searches of restaurants in at least three large cities. This information suggests that he was at least considering leaving. Do you know anything about his plans that you can share?"

The agent sat forward again, meeting each of their eyes, and nodded. "Mike was experiencing some anxiety. You likely noticed his high energy and intense focus over the years. These can be coping and avoiding strategies. Mike was deeply connected to the two of you and to Whisper Island. The island's ties to your father, Greg, were significant to him. However, the close-knit community eventually proved challenging for him. As Savor began to feel more routine, the coping strategies he had relied on seemed less effective. I will be honest with you," Agent Barrett said sadly, "I was strongly encouraging him to stay and work through it. I honestly can't tell you for sure what his decision would have been."

"I sense there is more to the story of Mike's original phone being found on Seal Island, but I respect that you feel you can't share that. I'd like your assurance again that Rheagan is safe," Greg said.

"You are correct, Greg, that there are aspects to this story I can't share, but likewise, it is not my intent to mislead you. Regarding your second point, I would like to reiterate that we believe Rheagan is indeed safe. This is a good segue into the next steps for you. Due to recent events and, again, in an abundance of caution, WITSEC will continue to monitor your situation. We would like two days to process your apartment and business, and then you are free to return. The sheriff's office will provide increased patrol security, but you are free to leave the resort now if you choose. Lastly, we will leave it to you and the sheriff's office to decide how you will characterize the break-in. Regarding the items in this box, our agency will retain the contents of the safe deposit box. With your permission, we would like to review your electronics and conduct a thorough search of all pertinent data. Afterward, we will professionally scrub the relevant searches and return the equipment to you."

Agent Barrett handed each of them a card. "If you have further questions related to the specifics of your situation, please feel free to give me a call," he said, rising from his seat to shake their hands again. His kind face looked drained, and Rheagan thought his life must not be an easy one.

She took a deep breath. "Agent Barrett, I can't thank you enough for coming here to Whisper Island. What you've explained today has helped with many questions, and I do feel that it will help over time." She turned to look at Greg, who nodded.

"Yes, we can't thank you enough, and for everything you've done for Mike over the years, too," he added.

They both shook Agent Barrett's hand and made their way outside. "I feel like some weight has lifted," Rheagan said, tipping her face up into the drizzling rain.

"So do I," said Greg, wrapping his arm around her shoulders as they walked toward his car.

Chapter Fifty-One

Before starting the car, Greg reached across to her and gently framed her face with his hands, his eyes focused on hers. "Let's get you checked out of the resort. I want to take you and Mr. Pickles back to my home. You'll be safe and more comfortable there. What do you say?"

"I would love that," she said, reaching toward him for a soft kiss.

It didn't take long to pack up the items she and Mr. Pickles had at the resort. The things she had recovered from her apartment earlier in the day were still in her RAV4, which she had left in front of her apartment when she had ridden with Greg to the sheriff's office.

As they prepared to check out of her room, a melancholy realization struck her, and she sat down suddenly on the edge of the bed.

"Honey, what is it?" Greg's expression reflected concern.

"I think I'm still processing so much information subconsciously, and it just occurred to me that we are now the keepers of secrets." She spoke slowly, and even to her own ears, her tone sounded lost.

"Help me understand." Greg settled down beside her on the bed's white duvet, reaching for her hand.

“This all started with Mike’s secrets, and now we have what we know of his secrets, and we have our own to add. The other day, out of the blue, Joe asked me what had happened to the safe-deposit key I found. I was startled by his question and told him it turned out to be nothing, probably just something Mike had found. And now, my guess is the sheriff will call the break-in a random “grab and toss,” so that will be another secret that I keep from my team at Savor, as well as from Kate and other friends. I know, I’m probably being melodramatic here … It just feels weird and sad.”

Greg pulled her into his arms and held her, pressing a kiss to the top of her head. “I get it now, and you’re right. You will have me to talk to, though,” he said, squeezing her shoulder before releasing her and looking down into her eyes.

Mr. Pickles gave a low-throated protest from his carrier across the room. Rheagan managed to laugh and shake off her mood. Reaching over to give Greg a quick kiss, she stood. “Thank you for hearing me out. Let’s get this show on the road.”

They decided to pick up her car on the way to Greg’s, and soon she and Mr. Pickles were easily settled in at Greg’s home. “It’s been a long day for you. You came all the way from Boise this morning,” Rheagan remarked as she began slicing cheese and toasting baguettes for their makeshift dinner.

“I wanted to be here for you and to meet with Sheriff Jansen and Agent Barrett. And … I have some news of my own that I want to share with you.” He had been pouring each of them a glass of wine, but now he turned and caught her questioning gaze. “Let’s wait until we sit,” he said, setting down the wine glasses and reaching for plates and cutlery for the island counter.

When they had taken their seats, he raised his glass to tap against hers, and after their first sip, he reached for her hand.

"Rheagan, the DNA test came back—I am not the father of Chrystal's baby."

Rheagan heard the sound of her own squeal, pure joy and relief. She jumped up to launch herself into his arms. He caught her against him and held her tightly. She thought she could feel relief in his embrace, too.

When she had returned to her seat, he reached for her hand again, looking deeply into her eyes. "Rheagan, I'm so glad we don't have to begin our life together working around a complication that I allowed to happen." He swallowed visibly and then went on. "I know our romantic relationship is still relatively new, but I know how I feel. I've had the benefit of getting to know you and seeing your character since Mike introduced us years ago. And now, with you on Whisper Island, and seeing and learning about you on my own, you have captivated me. I want a life with you." He swallowed again. "Am I rushing you?"

Rheagan could feel tears brimming in her eyes, and she focused on the steadying grip of his hands on hers. "I love you, Greg. I love your strength and your commitment to me. You've been such a rock, and I knew that I depended on you, but then …" she smiled up at him through her teary eyes, "that whole electricity thing started. You are not rushing me …"

Greg leaned over and captured her lips, giving her a long, promising kiss that ignited all that chemistry between them. "I'm going to follow this up with a ring, you know," he murmured against her lips, and she felt her own lips turn up in a smile.

Chapter Fifty-Two

Three days later, with Savor reopened, Rheagan sat down for a celebratory family dinner with her team. They had surprised her by making her a pizza. As a team, they had been practicing making pizzas from time to time, but until now, she had always been the one to handle the crust. Today, Manny was showing off his dough-tossing skills, and he was pretty good! He and Trey had coordinated on various flavor profiles, including a white pie with broccoli and garlic, which was delicious. They even served spicy mocktails with cucumber, cilantro, lemon, and serrano peppers to celebrate being back to work and her safe escape after the robbery.

At first, Rheagan found herself fighting a feeling of inauthenticity as she discussed the break-in. Still, she knew that she was providing the information as Sheriff Jansen had requested. There was nothing to be gained by making the community aware that mobsters from Philadelphia had visited their small island.

After lunch, Rheagan went upstairs to her office to handle some routine paperwork that had been delayed due to the temporary shutdown. Eventually, she found herself heading to the *Inspiration Room.* She sat down at the table and focused on Mike's CIA manual on the shelf in front of her, allowing herself again to feel that connection to him. *I loved you, Mike, but I am moving on now. I think you would want me to. Greg and I have talked a lot about how you were always such a "live in the moment" guy yourself, so we both feel you would want that for us. I hope you would be proud of Savor and of me. I've made changes that might not have been your choices, but they feel good to me, and I like to think you would understand.* Rheagan sat for a moment longer and then brushed the tears from her eyes.

On her way out of the room, she retrieved the CIA manual from the bookshelf and placed it gently on a higher shelf next to a small decorative pot with a vining ivy. Back in her own office, she opened her top drawer and removed the second insurance check from Mike that she had not yet cashed. She wanted to get Joe's feedback, but she had an idea.

Epilogue

Rheagan stepped outside into the darkness for a moment. She wanted to enjoy the view of Savor's presence from the sidewalk. Her restaurant looked warm and inviting, with deep-red awnings, brick accents, and glowing lights that welcomed guests into the cozy yet stylish interior. Tonight, Savor was filled with her closest friends and most loyal customers. Together, they were celebrating the opening of her separate yet connected Savor pizza bar, which featured a large domed pizza oven and a rustic bar with seating for customers seeking a more casual dining experience. The bar would also perform as the service bar for the original Savor's more formal dining room.

Her team had worked hard to help her realize her dream of creating the Italian version of Savor, and the pizza bar was more than she could have dreamed of. She was so proud of Joe as the new head chef of Savor. He and his girlfriend had recently moved into her former apartment above the restaurant, relieving Rheagan of the responsibility of being on-site twenty-four seven. Trey's skills as sous chef were the perfect complement to Joe's expertise, and Manny was thriving in his role managing the pizza bar. *I couldn't ask for a better team.*

The front door opened, and Greg came out. He walked over, pulled her close and pressed a kiss to the top of her head.

"I figured you were out here admiring the view. The restaurant looks exquisite," he said, smiling. "I'm very proud of you, Mrs. Andersen. You've made Savor an absolute success!"

"Thank you, but trust me, it's a team success. I'm incredibly proud of the entire team for all the new skills they've acquired and their dedication. And Greg, I couldn't have done this without your love and support. You mean everything to me." She reached up to press her lips against his, and his arms tightened around her. When the kiss ended, she looked playfully into his eyes and said, "I really appreciate your fast-tracking the zoning approval for Savor's pizza bar expansion, Mr. Mayor," she teased.

Greg laughed. "The office has to have some benefits to go along with all the meetings and paperwork."

"I am so very proud of you, Greg. You're already helping to modernize and create more opportunities for our community."

His gaze met her eyes as he said, "We are both lucky to be living our dreams and, with each other." Grabbing her hand, he smiled and led her back through Savor's front door. "Let's have another glass of champagne—this is a celebration!"

The End

About the Author

For years, Pamela Moulton, a certified public accountant, balanced a structured career in corporate tax with a creative mind filled with fictional characters. As you may suspect, the fictional characters ultimately won out, giving rise to her debut novel, *A Change to the Plan*. While she currently resides in Philadelphia, Pennsylvania, both *Whisper Island* and *A Change to the Plan* are set in the Pacific Northwest—a place where she once lived and still loves.

www.ingramcontent.com/pod-product-compliance
Lightning Source LLC
LaVergne TN
LVHW091126080826
845145LV00008B/2058

* 9 7 8 1 7 3 7 8 5 5 6 8 2 *